CW00524633

CHOSEN

OWENSEN WITCHES BOOK 1

DREIA WELLS

The characters and events portrayed in this book are fictional. Any similarity to real persons, living or dead, is coincidental and not intended by the author.

Cover design by: Undreia Capewell

Formatting by The Nutty Formatter

ACKNOWLEDGMENTS

I just want to thank my family for always having interesting stories to tell.
Thank you to my husband David for listening to me bounce ideas around and encouraging me to write this book.
I don't think I have ever written this much in my life, but now that I have, you're not getting rid of me.

An extra thank you to my sisters Tai and Fawn for being my ARC reader and all-around sounding board; without you pushing me, I wouldn't have finished.
Most of all, I want to thank my mother, who was never afraid to tell us a ghost story or two.
I love you all.

"I fear not the dark itself, but what may lurk within."
-Unknown

PROLOGUE

MAGNOLIA

May 1, 1920

She tried. She had tried for so long to forget her heritage. No, not heritage; her birthright. The one thing that made her who she really was, passed down from female to female in her family. "You're a witch, Mag, and that's what we were meant to be," her mother told her religiously. But for years now she had tried to ignore the urges and forget her visions that plagued her daily so that she and her family could lead a normal life. These were modern times, and the time of seer's and fortune tellers was over, she kept telling her husband. He was normal and she wanted to give him a normal life. He worked a normal job as a farmer on her family's land, and they had done well for themselves so far. They had managed to keep a low profile in their small town in Texas, and she was determined to keep it that way. Most people knew the history of her family, but over the generations it had all become hearsay, superstitions, and scary bedtime stories they told their children. But then they came. Those who wanted to destroy what she had built. Never. They would never have what rightfully belonged to her family. Blood of her ancestors soaked into the ground beneath her feet, and the dust of their bones in the very air she breathed. She wouldn't dare let the local townspeople take the land that didn't belong to them. But she had to get her children and her injured husband to safety, or they would have been killed if they were caught. This land belonged to her family long before others began to settle here hundreds of years ago but times had changes and the color of their skin deemed them unfit to own property in the eager eyes of their neighbors. Shaking herself from her thoughts, Mag opened her eyes as she stood in the clearing just outside the perimeter of her family's land. Her husband gravely injured, and her children sobbing quietly just a few feet away, she knew what she had to do. Mag dropped to her knees in prayer and stretched out her arms wide. She could feel her magic churning inside of her, but it wouldn't be enough for what she needed to do.

"I know you're there and you can hear me. Spirits of the earth and sky, light and darkness. Hear me now." Mag knew calling out in the middle of the night was not for the faint of heart. You never knew who would answer you in the dead of night. She was desperate, and she could still hear the shouts and cheers from those who had dragged them from their home in the distance. "Hear my plea, your daughter of light begs of you," she cried, as the sodden ground soaked into her nightdress. She listened as the winds began to shift around them and the clouds blocked out the moon shrouding the clearing in complete darkness. She sensed a presence.

"You called daughter of light." Mag didn't spook easily, but as she opened her eyes and gazed upon the depths of darkness, she knew there was no turning back. Nothing good would come from what she was about to do, but for her family and their ancestral land she would worry about the consequences later.

That night a deal was struck. One that would change the Owensen family forever. That night Mag danced, she danced with the devil.

1

NEV

....100 years later

I am gripping my steering wheel so tight; I think I might crack my knuckles. I don't remember pulling up into the driveway and shutting off my car. All I can hear are the faint sounds of Erykah Badu's 'Orange Moon' coming from the radio. Lifting my head from the wheel, I look up to see the shape of a man standing a few feet away from my car.

"I guess I didn't have a vision after all," I say out loud to no one. You know, all I wanted to do tonight was come home from a long day of dealing with other people's drama and put my feet up and watch some random mind-numbing tv. What I didn't expect was to turn down my street to complete darkness. There couldn't have been a power outage on just my street. Somehow, through muscle memory, I was able to find my drive, and here I was sitting in my car wondering why someone has decided to mess with me tonight. "Yes, that's how I got here," again I say to no one. Talking to myself is a regular occurrence, and I don't see myself losing that habit anytime soon. It is the way I cope. I should just turn the car back on, slowly back out, and get the hell out of here. Sleep be damned, I will get somewhere safe and phone my guardian, my cousin, or my sister witch.'

I look up again and see that the man is now standing at the hood of my car. "Shit." How had he managed to move so fast without me noticing, and why am I not getting the hell out of here? Putting my car in reverse and backing up a lot more quickly than I intended, I hit my brakes so hard my seatbelt is going to leave a mark. "Damn, that hurts." The man is there waiting like he doesn't have a care in the world. Did he just look at his nails like he was bored? You have got to be kidding me. I can feel my heart rate picking up, and my magic is ready to break free and go ape shit on this threat. I know I should make a phone call, but I will not be afraid; I am an Owensen, for crying out loud. I got this. I turn my car off and unbuckle my seatbelt, and as I grab the door— "Nevaeh," the man calls. The sound of his voice sends chills down my spine as I spiral into the depths of my memories.

"You called daughter of light." Mag looks up as his face begins to form before her eyes. His skin as black as night, as if he is pulling from the darkness itself. His eyes are black orbs, and his smile is so blinding with those unnaturally white teeth. He is beautiful, she thought as he stood above her in his black double-breasted pinstriped suit with blood-red buttons to match his colossal ruby red cufflinks he was now fixing in place. "Momma," her daughter cried from a few feet away. Hanita, her ten-year-old daughter, can see him as well, and she didn't expect that to happen so quickly. Her own magic manifesting on its own in a matter of minutes. She had tried so hard to shield her daughters, but not any longer. This was all going to happen now, whether she wanted it to or not. "It's ok, baby, take your brother and sisters and stay with your father," Mag tells her. Mag's eyes never leave the man in front of her as she stands quickly and slowly backs out of the clearing into the nearby trees. "Who are you?" she asks the man, who saunters over to her like he hasn't a care in the world.

"I think you know who and what I am, Magnolia. And I am

guessing you know exactly what you've done calling out for help in the dead of night. The darkness will always answer the call of desperation. So, tell me, Magnolia, what do you desire? Your husband is gravely injured, and we both know he won't make it out of this clearing. A mob has taken your family's land, and you have no one to help you. Pity you attempted to forget who you are and send your family's coven away. You would have no need of me, and I could be partaking of my night's delights."

"I don't need your lecture, demon," Mag yells as flames erupt from the pawn of her hand. If she knew she could kill him, she would have.

"Ah, there she is," he applauds her.

"I am many things, but a demon I am not. I don't have all night, but I am intrigued, Magnolia." He begins to step closer. "I have approached your family in many forms over the centuries, and I have never gotten this close, so as a sign of goodwill, I will heal your husband. But there will be a price, my dear; there is a deal to be made. Make your request before I get bored."

"But my family are light witches," Mag states to herself. She doesn't understand at this moment what he wanted with her family. But she knows it doesn't matter; she remembers her mother always saying, "What's done in the dark always comes to light." Shaking herself from that memory and dropping the fire-ball she is holding, she begins, "I want my family's land back, and for those who came on my land to pay for their crimes against me and mine. I want my family to be forgotten by the people in this community so that we can live undisturbed by those who want to persecute us." She looks up once more into the face of darkness and stares in the eyes.

He laughs. "Is that all? Don't you want more power? Don't you want to rule the magical world?"

"My family has enough power, but I am guessing you already know this. I have no desire to rule over anyone. I just want to make things right." Mag said to him, but by the grin on his face, he doesn't believe her.

Sighing, he bends down and knocks some dirt off his already immaculate wing-tip shoes. "Fine. It is done." Then he snaps his fingers.

All Mag hears in the distance are screams so horrifying she will never be able to forget them. "What did you do? Are you killing them? I didn't ask—"

"You asked for them to pay for their crimes against you and yours. I have done that. No one will remember the Owensen family in this community, and there is now a glamour around your land that no one will ever see or find unless they are an Owensen. Oh, and your husband is coming around as we speak."

"There is always a price for death and my family—" again, he cuts her off.

"Yes, for my fee, I would like to marry one of your daughters." Mag begins to protest, but he stops her. "Oh, Magnolia, I don't want Hanita, Sable, or Grace. I am talking about one of your future daughters, possibly one of theirs." He laughs. "I am definitely not interested in baby Thomas or any other males in your line. In fact, no more males will be born to this bloodline until I receive my prize. Your daughters will have a daughter, and their daughters will have daughters. I will have plenty of brides to choose from." He claps his hand and smiles that unnatural smile. "Your family will only become stronger with every generation, so who knows when or who I will choose. You all have such extraordinary gifts, Magnolia, and one of you will be powerful enough to rule at my side."

"You ask too much! You will take too much," Mag screams. "We are a family of healers and seers—"

"Yet here you are, holding a pure fireball in the palm of your hands. Fascinating, really, and let us not forget some of your own sisters are shapeshifters, and it has passed down to their children. And that lightning you hear in the distance, that is being created by your terrified eight-year-old daughter Sable. I can feel her magic from here. Light witches pretending to be light when you are not." He shakes his head and laughs. "Don't lie to yourself, Magnolia. I know who you are and what your

family can do." He turns in the direction of the clearing out of curiosity and begins to walk toward her family.

"Stop. We have a deal. Just don't take another step," Mag cries.

"Oh, no need to cry Magnolia, the deal was done when I snapped my fingers." And with that, he begins to vanish into the night from which he came. "I will be watching."

She could still hear his laugh on the wind when her husband ran in her direction.

"What did you do, Mag?" he screams. "What did you do?"

"Neveah," the voice calls again, shaking me out of the memory imprinted on my brain from the age of sixteen. We all received this memory of the deal that was struck to save my family almost one hundred years ago—a wonderful parting gift from my dear great, great grandmother Magnolia. But I've never had the gift of telepathy, so the fact that I can hear him in my head is freaking me out. Looking around for my phone, I call out to Siri to call Tia. Looking into the rear-view mirror, he still stands there like a psycho with this huge manic smile on his face. Talk about creepy. Pushing the speakerphone button on my phone, I keep my eyes on the mirror as she answers.

"Nev, are you ok?"

"Tia," my voice shakes with fear and anger. I can't believe this shit. "Tia, he's here."

2

TIA

"Who's there?" I say to Nev, who sounds terrified. I knew I should have just stayed home tonight. You ever have one of those feelings? Yep, I am having one right now.

"He is here, Tia. Standing at the bottom of the driveway, calling my name. He knows my name, Tia. He was in the front of the car, and when I tried to get away, he zapped himself behind me. So, you tell me who?" she screams into my ear.

I leave all my shopping and run toward the exit of the Target. Hey, don't judge me. I love Target.

"Don't move Nev, I am not that far away, and it will be faster if I shift to get to you," I tell her as calmly as I can.

"I can't believe I almost stepped outside my car—"

I don't let her finish. "You what?!" Stopping, I run my hair through my braids. Dang, my scalp hurts. Ugh. That's why I went to Target to buy braid sheen. Ok, getting off-topic here. I continue to listen.

"I thought that maybe he was some crazy warlock who thought he would torment me. I was about to show him he came for the wrong bitch! Until he said my name, Tia, and it triggered my memories. It was the same voice. Thank goodness we blessed both the houses and our cars," she whispers the last part.

"Look, I am going to send out an SOS to the family, and I'm going to have to leave my phone. Don't, for any reason, decide to be brave, Nev, and get out of the car. You cannot, I repeat, cannot fight him alone." I must find a way to get her out of this before he stops playing with his food and pounces.

I hang up the phone, open my car door and start stripping. Thank God, I decided to park on the side of the store out of the way so that I couldn't be seen. When I turned sixteen, I too received my great-great grandmother's memories of the deal she made a century ago, but I also shifted for the first time. My great grandfather Thomas was one of the last males born into our family before the deal. Usually, it was the males in our family that made the shift when they turned sixteen. But like Jeff Goldblum rightfully stated in Jurassic Park, "Life finds a way." Because great grandfather Thomas couldn't pass on his own shapeshifting abilities, they were passed down to his daughters instead. Initially, my great-great grandmother's plan was that the shapeshifters in our family would become guardians to the female witches. It would be the guardian's job to protect them as the first line of defense if the devil came a-knocking. But years past and the male shifters became fewer and fewer, and eventually, it became the task of the newly minted female shifters in our family to take up the mantel. It's not a hard job really, most of us end our duties after our "sister witch" gets married. Something to do with holy unions etc. etc. Once this happens, your guardianship ends, and you are free to find love yourself or take on another cousin, aunt, or sister. You're picking up what I am putting down, right? This shit is seriously mind-boggling.

The ironic part of this story, ladies and gentlemen, is that Neveah is engaged and soon to be married in a month. I love my cousin, but I was ready to begin my own life. I'm twenty-eight, for crying out loud.

Standing completely naked, I hide all my things under the

seat of my car, lock it up and hide my keys under the tire in the lockbox. Hey, let's just say this isn't my first rodeo.

Holding a breath and exhaling, I began to shift. Shifting for me is like putting on a mask. I visualize myself as my spirit animal, and she comes forth. Hey, did I mention I could fly? My spirit animal is a golden eagle, the biggest eagle in North America, and let me just say, considering there is magic involved, I am a whole lot bigger. You look up and see a bird the size of a Great Dane with a wingspan of ten feet and tell me you won't have nightmares. Launching myself into the air, I aim for our house a few miles away. Considering I can do up to 200mph at my fastest, I am not worried about taking longer to get there. Using my eagle-eye view, I notice our street is in total darkness, and the first thing I see is him, and he's looking right up at me. Thinking as quickly as possible and hoping Nev is sensing my presence, I circle around our house and dive straight toward the passenger side window.

This is either a good idea, or I am about to destroy some shit. As I get closer to the passenger side window, I can see Nev look up from her phone, and the look on her face is priceless. Scrabbling to let the windows down, I see she is aiming for the wrong one, and that is why I find myself shifting and face planting in the back seat of her car. Leaving my ass all up in the air.

"Take my coat." She throws it back on top of me as I sit up and put it over my very naked body.

"Why don't we have an emergency bag in the car for moments like this?" I ask sarcastically. Buttoning up the coat, I take a quick look back and nearly shift again at the sight of him just outside the back window.

"Geez, he is fast." I watch as he begins to walk in a circle around the car. Nev is getting anxious, and when she gets nervous, shit tends to burn. "Breathe, Nev, I am hoping that somehow we can come up with a plan to get into the house. If not, we are just going to have to wait here until morning." Climbing up into the car's passenger seat, I see that she is already melting her steering wheel, and her phone is scorched.

"Neveah, I think it's time for you and me to have a little chat," he singsongs.

"Yep, that's definitely him."

"What's the plan, Tia?" Nev asks. She hasn't taken her eyes off the vision in front of us. He's feeling himself standing there in an actual tuxedo and a silk dinner scarf around his neck. I mean, it's May in the south. Does the devil sweat?

"Tia," Nev shouts my name again. But I am just as transfixed. His skin is still as black as night, with the same maniacal smile on his face. It's so dark without the streetlights, but all I can see is his bright smile shining like a beacon. He's tall, standing about 6'4 with a body like a God. No, I can't call him a God, but he is a fallen angel, so…

"Ladies, I am not going to ask you to get out of the car, but we all know that if I wanted to get to you, I would have. Tia can't save you from me, Neveah. Why Magnolia thought shapeshifting "guardians" would protect you is laughable." He laughs, a nice deep, hearty laugh like he's at open mic night. Did he just air quote guardian like I'm nothing?

"You can call me Shade," he continues to talk to Nev, his eyes never leaving hers. "You've been chosen, my Neveah. You are my prize, and I have been waiting a very long time for you." he croons.

Turning to Nev, I feel her rage and know it won't be long before things get a little sketchy. I start to see movement in the darkness in the shape of enormous beasts closing in around the car and coming up behind Shade.

"The cavalry has arrived. Thank the heavens." I track their movements, but before they can get any closer, Shade snaps his fingers and laughs. You know I am getting really fucking tired of him laughing at us. I am itching to shift and rip him apart.

"Down girls," he says. All I can hear are growls and roars of frustration in the darkness.

"I think they're frozen." Nev finally shakes herself from his gaze and looks at me.

"Neveah, I didn't say you could look away," he calls out in anger, and the growls get louder all around us.

Neveah slowly turns her head toward this asshole, and her eyes are entirely black. "Nev, I am going to need you to breathe."

"Do you think I am going to comply?" Nev doesn't sound like herself, her voice loud and strong as it echoes into the night. Her hands begin to glow, and I know I need to be ready for anything.

Shade stays silent for a moment before he looks at her and smiles that damn, crazy-ass smile again.

"Oh, Neveah, I know you will. You have seven days."

And just like that, he's gone. The streetlights come to life, and I find myself staring at some very angry shifters.

3

SHADE

She resisted my compulsion. She is stronger than I thought. How exquisite! She must be new to telepathy; I don't think that that is one of her original affinities. She is a bag full of potential.

I have spent centuries searching for the witch who would tip the balance of power between light and darkness, and she is well within my reach. The Owensen's have always had a strong connection to their traditional source of magic and can conjure both light and dark magic. I have approached this family in many ways over the years and they refused me every time. So, I played the long game, and I watched from the shadows, and when the opportunity presented itself, I whispered into an ear and that's all it took to have the mob knocking down their door. A little racism goes a long way, I didn't make them do anything they didn't already want to do; I just pushed them along. Hey, I am the devil. So, when Magnolia called out in the night, I made sure I was the one who answered. Deal done! There is no such thing as a fair deal. Although, I thought I was getting rid of the shapeshifters in the bloodline, but I guess someone else had other ideas. I wonder who?

"Sir," my human servant calls in greeting as I walk into the door of one of my many dwellings. I plan to stay close and collect my prize on time. I can't chance anything going wrong in this transaction and considering she is only days away from getting married, I can't allow her to enter a holy union. Neveah is the one. She is the key to everything.

"She who is of earth and sky, fire and water, who sails across the skies. She is where our future lies. She who is truly blessed can maintain the balance between light and dark. If darkness intercedes and claims her with his mark, we are all lost. She will be lost for all eternity. Bringing forth chaos in her wake. Shrouding earth in darkness."

Leaning over the railing of my balcony overlooking the city, I remember the night I heard the Shaman speak her prophecy to her people. Her words echoing into the night as the fires rose high into the sky, I knew her words had purpose. I knew this prophecy was foretelling my future reign over the earth, and so I began to set the wheels in motion.

"Do you think he will allow you to see this through?" I was so lost in my thoughts I didn't hear him approach.

"Michael," I acknowledge, as I continue to look out over the city.

"Lucifer," he says with disgust.

"I prefer to be called Shade these days, it's a little more palatable, don't you agree."

"Call yourself what you like, Lucifer, but you do well to heed my warnings," he grits out. He always had a short temper.

"Neveah is not to be touched. You will let her marry and your deal with the Owensen family is over in the eyes of our father."

"How dare you come here and speak to me as if I will obey!" I feel myself changing and the shadow overtaking my human form. I continue to speak as the night itself. "A deal is a deal, or did you forget who and what I am. I answer to know one. I will rule over the humans, and I will take my bride and fulfill the prophecy," I say as I step out of the shadows and speak to him face to face.

"Tell me Michael since when has he ever interfered with my affairs here on earth? Why does it matter if I want to marry this witch?" I spit out.

"She is not yours to marry. Neveah is engaged to be married."

"A minor technicality," I say with a shrug.

"The balance must be maintained. You will never have dominion over humanity. Our father has given them free will for a reason, and you manipulated a deal in your favor. That will not stand." Michael's wings expand behind him, and he shoves off the balcony floor and hovers before me, in a golden glow with his sword blazing. What a showoff.

"Neveah is a light witch, pursuing her will be an act of war Lucifer. I will take great pleasure ridding the earth of you," he says as he takes his sword and points it down at me. I simply lean against the wall and cross my arms over my chest, waiting for his tantrum to be over.

"Careful brother, you are beginning to sound like me." I laugh.

"Careful brother for you overstep." Michael clearly didn't like my joke. Angels these days.

"You've just confirmed everything I need to know tonight, Mikey boy. Thank you. Tell Father… wait he can hear me. Father, she is mine," I say as I speak to the sky.

Michael laughs. "Dear brother, I should be thanking you." Putting the sword away, he flaps his wings. "Thank you for giving me a reason for war," he shouts and shoots off into the heavens.

"Not if I get her to the Underworld first," I say to the wind. Closing my eyes and feeling the shadows answering my call, I step into the void. I know what I must do.

I'm Lucifer and who said I had to be fair.

4

NEV

"Well, that was fun, ladies, but I would rather not do that again," Siobhan says as she walks through the front door of the house Tia, and I share. "I felt so exposed and a little too vulnerable being immobilized by his magic. It's making my wolf itchy just thinking about it," she continues while she grabs one of our blankets from the back of the couch and wraps it around her body.

"I don't know; I thought we could take him." Tia shrugs as she turns and locks the door. She loves to try to make light of every situation, and I have to say that I need a little bit of humor right now. Anything to take my mind off what just transpired. "I need clothes like now, my ass is out, and Nev, no offense, but this jacket does nothing for me." She laughs, opens the double doors, and walks down the hall to her room.

"I second that motion," Kes breathes out as she follows her sister down the hall. "I will grab us some clothes," she shouts back to Siobhan and Eddy.

"You know there ain't nothing in Tia's room that will fit my big ass, Kessandra," my cousin Eddy yells from the corner of the room.

"I will grab you something of mine, Eddy," I push off the wall I've been holding up against and head upstairs to my bedroom.

"It's going to be ok, Neveah; the Elders will know what to do," Siobhan sighs, wrapping the blanket tighter around her and sitting on the couch.

"I know, we will talk when I come back," I say without looking back. But what did I know? I have no idea how I am going to get out of this. I thought this would be over for me soon. Xavier and I are getting married in less than thirty days.

Oh, shit Xavier, I better call him tonight.

Who knows where I will be by the end of the night?

Focus Neveah.

Twenty-five years, I've kept my head down. I rarely use my magic except for training sessions that Tia and I hold together twice a month. I know I'm different, I can feel how strong my magic is, and it's getting harder to ignore it every day. I felt like I wanted to explode in the car, and my skin is still tingling from the aftershocks of it all. Maybe I shouldn't hold myself back anymore. I am going to need every ounce of it to get out of this mess. I'll be damned if I let him take me, literally damned.

Walking through my open-planned bedroom to the wardrobes along the wall, I catch a glimpse of myself in the mirror. Nothing's changed. My natural hair braided in a protective up-do style, dark brown eyes, caramel skin, and ocean waves of curves. Today, I looked amazing at the museum in my dark green, double-breasted pants suits and metallic gold ballet flats to match the shiny gold buttons. Hey, I don't do heels, and I am not about that life. I've always been a more voluptuous woman, especially in my family. We come in all shapes, sizes, and colors. We are all like a vast brown bag of skittles. Can I say taste the rainbow? I am not sure. "Brown-bow," I say out loud. Laughing to myself, I open the wardrobe and grab some jeans and a t-shirt for

Eddy. She will have to leave the girls hanging because I know my bras won't fit her.

Eddy is the only bear-shifter left in the family; most of us are birds, wolves, coyotes, and jaguars. She is naturally more considerable and taller than most of us here, unlike Siobhan and Kessandra— 'Kes'— have smaller frames like Tia. Now that I am thinking about it, I noticed Eddy doesn't look very happy downstairs. I guess a part of her might feel a bit of relief. She has been a guardian for so many of us over the years, and because her spirit animal is a bear, the elders decided she would continue her guardianship. When all the male shifters in our family passed on, it was up to the newly shifting females to become the protectors. Most of them guarded one or two sister witches before they could start their own families. But Eddy really wasn't given a choice. She was told it was her duty, and that was that. I can sense Eddy's resentment, and I get it; who wouldn't be tired after all these years.

Sending a quick text to Xavier, I turned and head back downstairs.

Nev: Call me ASAP. XX Nev.

Xavier: What's going on, sweetheart? Thought you would be watching all things TLC by now.

"What the hell are you talking about, Eddy? We are not just going to let him take Nev." I hear Tia shouting at Eddy from downstairs. Putting my phone in my pocket, I rush back downstairs. Eddy is facing off with Tia in the middle of the living room. I can't leave them for a minute without them jumping down each other's throats. Eddy and Tia don't get along that well, and it has everything to do with me. Eddy was chosen to be my guardian first, but a last-minute decision was made on my sixteenth birthday, and I went to Tia instead. To this day, I have no idea why it happened, but we never questioned the Elder's decision.

"Can you both just back off each other for a minute," I say to both as I shove clothes into Eddy's arms. That seems to get her focus on the fact that, yes, she is still naked. Snatching the clothes from me, she crosses the room, vanishes down the hallway, and slams a door. Did the house just shake?

"Nev, she wants us to just give you up," Kes says as she joins a freshly dressed Siobhan on the couch. "How selfish is she right now. We have to protect you and the other elemental witches of our family. Our duty. Neither of us agrees with that."

"Maybe you should," I say to them all. What the hell am I saying? I get the animosity from Eddy; she's been a guardian for a long time. At thirty-five, she is one of the oldest.

"She has no life, outside of being a guardian. She is looking after her sister's sixteen-year-old daughter Tamara now. When will it be over for her? So, I get it. I really do. Me being chosen; it saves all of you."

Do I want to give myself up? Hell no. But my family has suffered enough.

"We were so damn close," Tia says as she paces back and forth across the floor.

"But even if Nev was married, it would just be someone else. How long does this cycle continue? It took him one hundred years to pick her," Eddy says as she enters the room with a frustrated huff. "I know this is tough, but we all know the deal. We all knew that one day he would come for one of them."

"You don't have to be so fucking smug about it, Eddy," Tia growls out.

"There just has to be away. The Elders have been working on a way to get us out of this for years. They have to have a plan," Siobhan said. "Now that we know he has chosen Neveah; we focus our energies on her." I notice the disgust on Eddy's face at what Siobhan just said, but as soon as she saw me look her way, the expression was gone. What the hell was that about?

Everyone's phone starts to ring at once, and we all scramble to answer.

"Hello," we all say at the same time. Jinx!

"Nev, when you didn't text me back, I was worried. What is going on, baby?" Xavier rushes to say to me.

"Xavier, he came for me tonight," I paused and sighed. "He

chose me," I say as I swallow a lump in my throat. Damn, I could use some water right now.

"What do you mean—"

"The devil has come to collect, and he decided he wants me," I cut him off as I turn and head toward the kitchen.

"I am coming to you now," Xavier says. I can hear him grabbing his keys, and I know it is not the best idea for him to come to me right now. The last thing I need is for Shade to find him first and use him to get to me.

"Xavier, there is nothing you can do. We don't know what our next move will be, and I guarantee we will hear from my mother very soon," I say to calm him, but I can still hear him moving. Damn it, Xavier, don't try to be a hero. Once Xavier proposed to me a year ago, he was told about who my family was and what it meant to marry an Owensen woman. It is not the most straightforward conversation to have with "normal" humans. Especially when they are told about the deal that was struck with 'he who must not be named. Harry Potter is life! Anyway, back on topic, the last thing I need is for my very human fiancée to get killed trying to save me from something he doesn't understand.

"Nev, I need to tell you something," he says almost too quietly.

Just as I was about to ask him to repeat himself, Tia runs into the room.

"Tell Xavier we are all going to Owensen Manor," she says as she turns and walks away.

"Xavier, we are going home. Meet us there. I love you."

"Nev, I don't know where Owensen Manor. Every time I've been there, I can't seem to remember the exact location," he says in a panic—another security measure put in place by the Elder witches of the Owensen family.

"Don't worry, Xavier, once you get close enough, I will find you."

5

XAVIER

Keys in hand, I head to the door of my flat.

"I am going to need clothes," I say to myself.

Running to my bedroom, I grab my gym bag and dump the content of my gym clothes onto my bed. That's going to need a wash. Thinking it over, I grab the laundry basket and swipe the clothes into it and toss it in the corner. I try to keep my mind off Nev and just focus on getting to her as fast as I can. With my bag now packed, I head toward the door, wondering whether I should have insisted she listens to me just now. I had something to tell her that I am sure will change everything about our relationship. I had tried to say to her so many times before and when we first met; I didn't think it was important because it was my job to protect her from afar. I was told that there was no way I should reveal myself unless it was necessary because it would mean her life depended on it. But I love her. We fell in love, and at the time, marrying her would end my assignment, and we could live our lives together; she would be safe, and I could tell her about me in my own time.

I am not supposed to exist. I should have been killed or not allowed to have been born, apparently. The thing is, I am a one-hundred-and-fifty-year-old Nephilim and son of Archangel Raphael. I was hidden for a very long time until I decided that I could serve a purpose here on earth. The Heavenly Father allowed Raphael to keep me, and he made sure that my mother and I were kept safe and cared for. To make a very long story short, he appeared to her after my mother escaped her then-husband; beaten, broken, and near death, and he saved her. Instead of granting her healing and going on his way, he continued to visit her, and eventually, they fell in love. I was a product of their passion. I had only met my father a few times in my life so that he could teach me how to cope with my 'angelic gifts' that were passed on to me.

I didn't have wings. Damn, I wished I could fly. But I could teleport like a boss.

Five years ago, I was approached by my father and Gabriel and given the task to watch over Neveah. I worked as a doctor in the local hospital near her and stayed in the shadows, watching from afar. My father, the "Master Healer," passed on his healing powers to me, so working as a doctor came naturally. I knew that she already had a guardian, but I was the 'in case of emergency, secondary plan. It was all worked out perfectly until two years ago when Neveah was out shopping and was accosted by strangers. I intervened and chased the men away without using my powers, and that is how we met. I knew I couldn't go back to the way things were, and now here we are, days from being married.

I hid who I was from her, and it kills me every day that I was dishonest. But there was no other way. Now she needs to know; her life depends on it.

Of course, he goes and chooses her! Lucifer can't have what's already mine. I can't allow it to happen.

Quickly locking my flat up and heading to my car, I glance around at my surroundings. If I could teleport right now, I would, but with all the enchantments placed on Neveah's family's manor, I would never be able to get in.

So, the car it is.

6

NEV

It didn't take us long to get on the road after my mother sent out an all-family alert. Eddy, Siobhan, and Kes shifted and left to go and retrieve the sister witch under their protection. We would all meet at the manor later. Tia flew back to her car, and by the time she returned, I had our 'to go' bags ready. It's been ingrained in us to always have a bag packed for emergencies just like this. I just can't believe I am the reason for it.

"So, what's the plan? I can almost see the wheels turning in that brain of yours." Tia looks over quickly from the driver's side of the car.

"I just want everyone to make it to the manor safely, and then we can see what the Elder's plan of action will be. All I do know is that this cannot be the end for me," I say as I turn my head to stare out the window. Placing my head in hand, I suddenly catch movement out of my peripheral. Something is out there, moving in the darkness. Even with Tia driving as fast as she is, I can just make out shapes in the night.

"Don't worry, Nev, I won't let him get to you. That's a promise."

"A promise that you can't keep," I snap back at her. Breathe Neveah. I feel my magic rising inside of me. Something is wrong.

"Tia," I say softly. Trying not to panic her while she is driving.

"Look, we've been driving for an hour now, and it's almost two a.m. I am going to ignore the attitude because no one expected this to happen tonight. We will fight to save you from this fate, Neveah. There is no way in hell you're going to be dragged to the Underworld without one. No need to apologize," she says to me quickly.

Closing my eyes, I focus on the world around us. Slowly, I can sense what's following us in the woods on either side of the road. All of them.

Shadow demons.

Of course, he wasn't going to make this journey easy on us. Seven days my ass.

"Tia, drive faster."

7

XAVIER

Looking at the time on the dashboard, it is almost two a.m. I hope that Tia's got Neveah to Owensen Manor by now. I am not that far away from the small town in which her family lives, and hopefully, she will be awake to instruct me the rest of the way.

"Xavier!"

My father pulls me out of my train of thoughts, and I almost run off the road. I really hate when they appear out of nowhere.

"A little warning, please, I could have hurt someone," I say as I steady my car. Yep, that person just shot me the finger for almost hitting them.

"My sincere apologies Xavier, but there is not a lot of time, and you will need to act fast. Neveah and her guardian are about to be attacked."

"The Manor is under attack? I thought there were protections—"

"They are still on the road but still not close enough to the manor. Lucifer did not listen to Michael's warning, and we think he will try to intercept her before his seven-days expire. If he gets her to the Underworld, she will be lost to us."

"Michael's warnings, am I missing something here?" I question him. I never ask too many questions of my father. I have always been a good soldier, and I do as I'm told, but I don't think I have been privy to all the information.

"Father, I need you to explain." I quickly glance over to the passenger side and see he is agitated by my saying this.

"There is no time, Xavier!" he insists.

"Explain," I shout. I don't want to be left in the dark regarding Neveah, I need to know what's happening, and I need to know now.

"Xavier, I will explain later. I promise you this, son. But right now, I need you to teleport to Neveah, get her to the manor before they are overrun by the Shadows."

"Shadow Demons?" I ask.

"Yes, it seems Lucifer has summoned them to grab Neveah and bring her back to him. He wouldn't dare appear to try to grab her himself, not now anyway."

"He's testing her strength," I say to him as I pull my car over.

"She is stronger than he knows my son and getting stronger. There is so much Neveah needs to learn about her power and herself. Now go. She will need you." He reaches over, grabs my shoulder, and briefly smiles. His touch allows me to catch a glimpse of Neveah's family manor location and the memories all come back to me.

"I am sorry she has to find out about you this way. I wish there was a way to make this easier. But it seems we are out of time," he says quickly, and then he's gone.

And so am I.

8

TIA

"Shit," I yell.

Thank goodness for seatbelts as I throw us both forward, hitting the brake hard. All I can see in the middle of the road are hundreds of floating red eyes. Looking both left and right, I can see the darkness closing in on my car, and slowly the figures emerge from the woods. They move randomly as they break out of the darkness that holds them. They had black humanoid figures with extremely long arms and legs, sharp claw-like daggers for fingers, and those creepy as hell bright red glowing eyes. Shadow demons are malignant spirits who are stuck between realms unable to pass on. I wouldn't want to run into one if I could avoid it, but this is a hoard.

"Tia, we are going to have to fight; there is no way out of this," Neveah says, and I watch both her hands light up in flames.

"I could shift and carry you if I have to, Nev." I will keep her from harm no matter the price. It is what we've been taught from day one.

"We won't make it, Tia. You can shift and fly out of here and get help. I can hold them off."

"I am not leaving you, Nev!" I shout at her. "We do this together, alright?" I turn to look at her as she nods quickly and brings her hands together in prayer, turning them slowly as she creates the most gigantic fireball I have ever seen. Nev shoots both hands out quickly, and the force of the fireball blows both car doors into the shadow demons on either side, giving us clearance to step out into the night.

I step out and shift quickly. Well, there went another one of my favorite shirts.

I take flight, making a tight circle around the car using my wings to push back the demons and create a path for Nev, who's blasting demons with fireballs left and right. I am not sure how long she can keep this up, but she has never had to sustain her fire for this long.

I hover over her and continue to use my wings to keep as many of them back as I can. I alternate between flying and hovering for a few minutes. I can't see an end in sight.

Suddenly Nev's head falls back, and her eyes begin to glow white; her flames begin to take on the same color. She screams and, like a bomb going off, shoots out a molten burning flame, decimating the shadow demons all around us.

"Well, that's new," I say to myself.

Nev looks at her hands, then up at me as if she could read my mind. I watch as her eyes close and she begins to fall.

I swoop down to grab her, but before I can reach her, Xavier appears out of thin air and catches her before she hits the ground.

Again, that is new.

"Xavier," I barely hear her say as she strokes his face then passes out completely.

"Xavier, where the hell did you come from? How did you just do that?" I touch down, shift, and walk over to him, cradling her in his arms.

Wait. I'm naked. But that doesn't matter because I need answers.

"Tia, when have to go now, more are coming. I can feel it. You can shift back and fly to the manor. I will meet you there with Nev," he says, taking no notice of me at all as he continues to scan the area around us.

"Teleport? Xavier, you have a lot of explaining to do. I won't leave her." I mean, come on, this is just too much crazy for one night. Quickly looking at my black burnt-out car and the smoke rising from it, I realize there is no way I will be able to write that off. My car, I think to myself.

"Trust me, Tia, I will get her there," he pleads with me. But I don't get a chance to argue with him because I can see the darkness gathering again.

"Shift Tia, and go," he yells.

I don't waste time looking back as I shoot into the air and take flight toward the manor.

Xavier and Nev are already gone.

He definitely has some explaining to do.

9

NEV

I wake up to darkness with a migraine worthy headache. Whatever happened to me back there on the road completely drained me. I don't know how Tia got me out of there, but wait I vaguely remember seeing Xavier before the lights went out. That's not possible—

"Neveah," Xavier says from somewhere in the room. The sound of his voice soothes me and eases tension I didn't know I was holding on to.

"Xavier, how are you here? How were you out on the road tonight?" I ask as I try to sit up, but the room instantly starts to spin.

"Here let me help you," he says as he rushes over to me and helps me prop up on some pillows. He turns on the lamp on the nightstand and I squint in the glow of the soft light.

My head is pounding. Ugh, I overdid it tonight.

Xavier sits on the side of the bed and takes my head in his hands; all I can do is stare into those bright hazel eyes and the smooth tawny skin of his face.

He is beautiful. He is mine.

His hands are glowing, and I feel so serene as my vision clears and my headache is completely gone. Shaking myself from this tremendous sense of calm washing over me, I am instantly brought back to the here and now. Looking around the room as the lamp on the side table casts a soft glow over the bedroom, I know I am in my mother's wing of the manor. I am propped up on crisp white pillows with embroidered cases, that I am sure were made years ago by someone in my family. In the middle of the room is the huge mahogany four poster with intricately carved eagles, bears and cats circling around. This room is warm and comfortable, with a hint of contemporary and a huge fifty-five-inch flat screen on the wall on the opposite side. Finished with my appraisal of my mother's recent updates, I turn to look at my fiancée for the first time with new eyes.

"Xavier, how is this possible?" I ask as I pull away from him. The past few hours are beginning to weigh heavily on my mind, and I don't know if I can take much more. I just need to keep it together a little longer before I fall to pieces later.

"Nev, there is a lot I need to tell you. Let me explain it all to you please," he says and reaches for my hands.

"No, what are you? How are we here? Did Tia bring me here? How did you just take away my pain?" I ask in rapid succession.

"Neveah, I am a Nephilim. I—"

"Nephilim?" As in Angel/human hybrid. I don't know much about them, but I thought they didn't exist anymore or better yet weren't allowed to exist. My fiancée is part angel, and I had no idea. Well, my mind is completely blown. How did I not know?

"Why didn't you tell me?" I ask him. "Wait, no better yet, why can't I sense your magic?"

"Because I couldn't. To answer the second part of your question, I have been shielding my magic from you. Believe me when I say to you that there was no malicious intent and that I did what I had to do to keep you safe. Neveah, I have been watching out for you for a very long time. My father and the archangel Michael gave me the task of protecting you from afar.

I have been doing so for five years now." He pauses, and I guess it's to see if I am going to ask more questions, but at this moment I am at a loss.

Sighing he continues.

"Do you remember two years ago the night we met?" he asks me, eyes searching mine.

"Of course, you saved me from those two assholes who tried to assault me." Remembering the night, I met Xavier was easy to recall, I had just returned to my car when two men came out of nowhere and started to harass me. Before I could even blast them with my mojo—because they both had no idea what they were up against—Xavier stormed down the road like a dark knight and saved the day. Now that I think about it, there was no one else around and it seemed as if he came out of the ether. At the time I didn't think anything of it, considering I was more relieved I didn't have to use my magic to put those jerks in their place.

"Well, that night I revealed myself to you and everything changed. I wasn't supposed to reveal myself. My task was only to watch from a distance and only step in when Tia couldn't. When I saw how distressed you were and the way you started to respond to the men around you, I knew I had to jump in before something big happened. You are a very strong witch Nev and even back then I could see sparks flying from your hands before they even noticed."

"I can control myself, Xavier!" I am getting a bit salty from that last statement. I wouldn't have killed those men. Maimed maybe, killed never. It is not in my nature to be that aggressive, even when I feel like I am about to erupt like a volcano most of the time. My mind takes me back to the white flames and the white explosion out on the road tonight, and I look at my own hands in a new light.

I don't know whether to be raging mad that he lied, grateful for the divine blessing of having angelic protection, or again raging mad. Five years, so that means he was a creepy stalker for three of those years without me having a clue. Is our wedding real? I think to myself, and I feel sick to my stomach just thinking about it. One way to find out.

"Is this real between us?" I ask him out loud, but I am almost afraid of this answer.

"I love you, Neveah. I fell in love with you before I even revealed myself to you. You're everything to me and I will do anything, go anywhere to protect you." I believe him, and that serenity and calm from earlier spreads over me like a warm blanket. I realized then that this is what his magic feels like and what he had been shielding from me all this time.

"I can feel your magic now," I say to him with a little wonder in my voice.

"I know you're upset with me Neveah I can feel it. I wanted to tell, but the Angels didn't know Lucifer would move this fast. They thought that once we were married, he wouldn't consider you—"

"And the cycle continues," I say as I move over to the other side of the bed and stand up. The last thing I want is for this to continue down the line. There must be an endgame. My family can't continue to go on this way. I think about Eddy and I truly understand her emotions for the first time. I clench my fist and I feel my magic recharging me and lighting the fires underneath my skin. We are all tired and weary of it all. This shit ends with me.

"Xavier, I love you." I turned and faced him after I took a minute to collect myself. I look at him and I don't feel betrayed, but exhausted, heavy and weighed down by my circumstances, yep definitely. I don't know what the heavenly father was playing at, but Xavier is in my life for a reason, and we will see this through. I can feel his magic as it washes over me again, reassuring me that this is right. As much as I want to be upset, I just can't find it in myself to be.

Xavier crosses over to me and I meet him halfway as he gathers me in his arms, and I cling to him and just for a moment nothing matters and it's just us. I take this moment and no more because something tells me it only gets harder from here on.

As if he could read my mind, Xavier places a single lingering kiss on my forehead and leans into me. "We are going to get through this. I will not let him have you," he says softly. That is the second time I have heard this tonight and as much as I want to believe it, I know nothing is promised.

We are quickly interrupted by someone pounding on the door, sighing I look toward it and count to three.

No, not someone, but Tia as she opens the door in a rush and crosses over to Xavier in a few angry strides and gets in his face. Baring her teeth at him she growls impatiently as she places herself between, he and I. "Explain," she growls again, and I can almost see her eagle itching to get out. Moving from behind her, I place my hands on both her shoulders and slowly back her away from Xavier.

"Tia, I am ok. You can see that I am not harmed and in one piece," I say calmly to her. She takes a breath, and I can physically see her spirit animal settle.

"You didn't see what I saw, Nev. For the first time in my life, I was afraid. We were in a tight spot back there and here comes Xavier out of nowhere. I need answers," she says as she glares at Xavier over my shoulder.

"Xavier is a Nephilim," I say quickly, before she gets agitated again.

"Wait, he's a what?" She looks at me once more.

10

TIA

"So, let me get this straight, you're Nephilim and your father is the actual Archangel Raphael?" I say as Neveah recounts all the information Xavier had told her earlier. I mean, you can't make this shit up. This is some straight up Urban Fantasy type stuff, and I feel like I just fell down the damn rabbit hole of stories. I slide down the wall I was holding myself up on and sit on the floor, resting my hands on my knees. I just feel tired and looking up at Nev I can tell she is feeling it too. Granted, we have yet to go to bed, and by sound of my Aunt Willa's voice on the way to see Nev I don't think we are going to get any rest any time soon.

"Your mom has called a family meeting in the great room." I look up at them both, I hadn't noticed Nev had gravitated back over to him. As soon as I rushed through the door, a few minutes ago, I was hit in the face by his power. So calm and serene, he didn't even flinch when I got all up in his face. How the hell did he manage to shield himself from us for this long? My spirit animal peeks out through my eyes and scans him for herself. His aura is the purest blue I have ever seen. Finally, accepting that he is no danger to us my animal recedes, and my vision goes back to normal.

"I guess we better get this over with then," Nev states as she crosses over to me and holds out her hand to help me up.

"Well, Xavier, you ready for the biggest family freak out of all time? Wait, just being in the room with you will calm everyone down a bit, but the elders probably feel your magic already. I don't even know how you were able to cross over the enchantments and shields around the manor." I look at him and head through the door of the bedroom with them following behind me.

"My father gave me the exact location when he warned me that you two were in danger. Do you think the elders already know about me?" he says to no one in particular.

"I am so sick of secrets! What the hell is wrong with this family? If they did know, they acted none the wiser. They must have known what you were, and they were ok with you two getting married without any real vetting. The elder's vet every male who marries into this family, it's very intense. I thought it was because you were a doctor etc.," I say as I continue down the long corridor of Aunt Sable's wing of the manor. I turn around when I don't hear them moving anymore and see that Neveah is getting upset by my speculation. I mean, I am not 100% sure of this, but all the evidence points to them knowing about Xavier.

"So, that means they've talked to the Archangels. There is still a lot that I even don't know," Xavier says with just a hint of irritation.

"I just want to know the whole truth." Nev sounds weary and barely keeping herself in control.

"We are going to get you answers, Nev," I say, as I continue to make my way out of this wing of the manor. Damn, this place is huge.

Our family's manor is an accumulation of all the wealth we've made through our many businesses throughout the magical communities. Yes, communities. We might be hidden in this small town, but the magical world knows exactly who and what we are.

64,500-square-foot Tudor Revival. Let's just say great, great grandmother Magnolia had a thing for Shakespeare. It was built in 1915, red brick exterior, steeply pitched roofs, and I can't even tell you how many chimneys. Four wings were built off the main house—that would eventually house all the different families of her four children. Hanita, Sable, Grace, and my great grandfather Thomas. Technically we are only all here when the family is celebrating something—big weddings, funeral, rituals, and of course holidays. This is the first time we've had an all-out-family emergency.

If anything, it will be one hell of a meeting and to think I was going to spend my night watching *Vikings* and loosening my braids with braid sheen. Living the dream, Tia. I laugh at my own mental musings and start down the large center staircase that leads to the main house.

We can hear all the family gathering in the great room as we approach. I turn to look back at Neveah and Xavier, and just for a minute, I feared for their future together. None of us knew the outcome of the next seven days. All I can hope for is that we would all do our damnedest to keep Nev here, safe with us. Taking a breath and turning the corner, I almost collide with my sister Kes.

"I was just about to run up and get you guys," she says to us, but her eyes instantly lock with Xavier's, and she opens her mouth again, but I cut her off.

"Look, it's a surprise to us all and by the look on your face the elders have already told everyone what and who Xavier is," I say quickly before she can launch into a thousand questions.

"Let's get this over with so we can get some sleep."

At the mention of sleep I yawn, Kes follows, and so do Nev and Xavier. I laugh and steer my sister back into the room.

I just want this night/morning to end with me staring at the back of my eyelids.

11

NEV

As soon as we cross into the room, the entire family turns to watch us approach. You could hear a pin drop with how quiet the room became. I can feel their eyes and as I look at some of them, I can see it written all over their faces.

Pity. Sadness. Relief. Well, they can have all that shit. Ugh, I need a cup of coffee if I am going to get through this, but nothing seems to be going my way tonight. Well, take that back it is now morning, I can see the light of predawn through the floor to ceiling windows on the far side of the room.

"We better grab a seat in the back to stop people from turning around and staring," Kes whispers to us as she walks to the back of the great room. But of course, even that is too much to ask for.

The Great room is huge with a high ceiling to accommodate the two massive glass chandeliers hanging from the center. The elders are all sitting around the massive fireplace, the focal point of the room and the rest of the family it appears, have all taken up residence on the nice comfy couches lining the walls. Leaving us to sit in the armchairs strategically placed in the middle of the room. The Elders of our family consist of the first-born daughters of the descendants of Mag's four children. My mother Willa is the eldest, Tia and Kes's mother Aunt Joy, Aunt Penny, and Siobhan's mother Edina. Our dads stand behind their wives dutifully, like pillars of strength holding up the family, they are the glue that keeps it all running smoothly. As we move to our seats, I look up into my father's eyes and he smiles softly back at me with a promise that he will talk to me after all this is over. It gives me comfort knowing that whatever happens he will be there to embrace me and tell me it will all be ok. Even if it's not. My mother has always been about duty, obligation, and maintaining our magical standing in the world. I don't know if there is a nurturing bone in her body. I know she loves me and my little sister Tempest, but it is always my dad who gives out the hugs and kisses.

She doesn't even look over at me as she stands now to address us all. *Hello, to you too Mother,* I think to myself. I guess she is going to handle this like she does her weekly board meeting and not as if anyone's life is on the line.

"Family, I have called us all home so that you are all under the veil of protection against the danger that we now face. Last night Shade appeared to my daughter Neveah and has chosen her as his bride. She has been told she has seven days before he returns to collect her, but we all know the cunning of the devil. He has already sent shadow demons to intercept Nev and Tia on the way here. He had no intention of waiting."

The entire room erupts in chaos. Everyone is talking at the same time.

My mother uses her magic to amplify her voice to quieten everyone down and bring the focus back to her. "As you can see Neveah and Tia are safe and sound. We must give our thanks to Nev's fiancée Xavier, son of Raphael, for saving them at the last minute and whisking Nev here before they were overcome," she says as she finally turns her head toward us and smiles. I am instantly livid. She knew about Xavier somehow, and she has a lot of explaining to do. I need answers damn it. Xavier and I both do.

Again, the room erupts in chaos. At this rate we won't finish this meeting until lunch time.

She raises her voice and quiets everyone.

"So, what are we going to do?" I hear Siobhan ask from the back of the room. I turn around and look at her and Eddy sitting on the couch near the back wall with their sister witches sandwiched between them. How Tamara is sleeping through all the commotion I have no clue, but I am envious of her in this moment.

"Daughter, you talk out of turn," my Aunt Edina says to Siobhan.

"Thank you, Edina," my mother states. "To answer your question niece, we are going to continue with the plans to marry Neveah and Xavier. The wedding will take place this Friday. Once she is married, this will all go away. Shade will no longer have a target and we can move on with our lives," she says with strong conviction, but I was looking for it, that little flicker of doubt that flashed across her face. Gone in an instant, but it was there.

You have got to be kidding me. Is this the solution the Elders have come up with? I turn to look at Tia and Kes, then back at Siobhan and Eddy in shock. I came here thinking there would really be an actual solution. I jump to my feet and feel my magic stirring inside me. My emotions feeding my magic like kindling, I pull away from Xavier and clinch my hands into fists. *Come on Nev, control yourself,* I say to myself.

"You know as well as I do that marrying Xavier is not going to stop him from coming for me, Mother. We can't just keep kicking the proverbial can down the road and hope he chooses someone else. I know that there is more to this story that you are not telling us in this room. When will it end? We all sit and wait on tenterhooks, wondering when someone will be chosen. We have all spent our lives looking over our shoulders, never really living because of a deal made one-hundred-years ago. Well, I call bullshit to that. Do you think you can trick a trickster? How the hell do you think he manipulated great, great grandmother Mag all those years ago? Don't you think he hasn't spent years biding his time, knowing that when he appeared, we would resist?" I say to not only my mother, but to everyone in the room.

"Neveah, I understand this a very emotional time for you, but we have your best interest at heart." My mother seems to soften just a little bit so that I will calm down. But I will not. I look at her and turn my back on the Elders and I address the room. Boy, I am breaking all protocols this morning, but this is what happens when I don't sleep, and I haven't had a cup of coffee.

Everyone in the room gasps.

"There is only one solution to this problem. We find a way out of this deal. We break the chains that have been holding our family hostage all these years. I refuse to watch another witch give up her life for something none of us agree to," I say to them all. I have got their attention. If anything, they all have thought this exact same thing. I look directly at Eddy, and I can see her eyes darting across the room as if she can't look at me. *What's that about, I wonder? Maybe she's reflecting on what she said earlier. We can square it away later;* I think as I continue my rant.

I turn back to face my mother and the Elders, and I know by the looks on their faces they are not happy with my little outburst. Well, tough. It's time for some hard truths, and it's time for me to lay it all on the line.

"So, if you want to plan a wedding Mother, plan it. I know that there is more to this than just marriage." *There it is again, that flash of doubt on my mother's face.* "But if I must, I will walk right out of those gates and give myself over to him, if by the end of the week there is no other way to break this deal. This curse, because that's what this is… A curse, and it ends with me." With that said, I turn and walk right out of the doors of the great room without looking back.

12

NEV

I need to think, and I need to sleep. Coffee. Not in that order exactly, but all three of those things are on the to do list. As soon as I left the room, all hell broke loose, but I didn't stop and really, I didn't care to hear any more of what my mother had to say. I said my piece and now I need some peace and quiet to figure out my next move. Taking myself up the stairs my legs feel like lead weights are attached to them, the exhaustion is pressing down hard. The way I used my magic fighting the shadow demons has taken its toll on. I mean, what was going on with my flames? White flames shot out of my hands last night and I obliterated them all. Something new to add to my list of growing elemental abilities, but this felt like something different inside of me. I felt so angry at what was happening to us back there on the road; I felt angry for my family and the burden we've all had to bear for so long, it just all came out of me. Stopping at the top of the stairs, I call on my fire, making sure I stay away from the antique wooden staircase. The last thing I need is to burn down the house around us. With my hands outstretched in front of me, I reach with my left hand and the flame is your typical orange-yellow flicker, so nothing new there. I reach with my right hand and almost grab the rail to stop myself from stumbling. In my right hand the flame is bright white with black shadows flickering throughout. What the actual hell is going on? I stare down at both hands, one orange and one white, and instantly shake them both—as if I've been burned—tucking them under my arms, I continue my journey back to my room. I am sure there is a reasonable explanation for what is happening to me. My only thoughts are that maybe I was so freaked out about fighting demons and getting myself and Tia safe, that my magic just went a bit haywire.

Do you really believe your broken?

I stop walking. Am I really that tired that I am hearing voices in my head?

Neveah, I am very real. You have so much power and I want to show you all that you are capable of. All that we both can achieve together.

Ok, so I'm not crazy and I know that voice. It was in my head last night. Shade. Lucifer. The Devil was in my head talking to me, as if he was walking right next to me. How is that even possible?

We are connected now that you are my chosen. You will be mine and there is nothing you can do to stop this. A deal is a deal.

Yeah, a deal I am sure you manipulated Magnolia into making happen. I refuse to believe that the events that led up to the deal didn't have your infamous hand in it.

Well, you are a clever girl, Neveah. How else was I to get what I wanted? It took me years to finally get an Owensen on board with what I have planned.

And that is? What is it they say in movies about the bad guy? Oh yea, you keep them talking long enough for them to give it all away. I hear him laughing in my head.

You have six days, Neveah.

Well shit. And just like that, he's gone.

So, coffee, sleep, think, and figure out how to keep Shade out of my head. How am I still upright? I must still be in shock. He was in my head and now we are connected because I am his chosen. Good grief.

Fuck my life.

Finally making it back to my room, I make quick work of undressing only to remember that all my clothes from my emergency bag are literal ashes on the road. I could go to Tempest's room and grab something from, but I can't take another step. Climbing in the bed with just a bra and panties, I cover myself with the blankets and instantly relax and close my eyes.

Right before I drift off, I hear the door open and movement from the side of the bed. I can feel that it's Xavier, his presence only calms me further and sleep is not that far off. He climbs in the bed beside me and lies on top of the blanket, pulling me close and tucking me beside him. That is the last thing I remember before sleep took me.

13

NEV

I wake up to knocking on the door. I just can't find it in my heart to open my eyes, let alone get up and walk over to open the door. I feel the bed dip and pry my eyes open to see Xavier crossing over to the door. My beautiful fiancée is still fully dressed and despite everything that happened only a few hours ago, he still looks so well put together. Must be a half-angel thing, I think to myself as I sit up, bringing the covers over me.

"I bought Nev some clothes. Tia says everything they had burned in her car last night," my sister Tempest says to Xavier.

Oh crap, Tia's car. Tia loves her car, and it didn't stand a chance when I blasted the hell out of those Shadow demons last night.

"I managed to scramble some things together for you too, Xavier," she says, bringing me back from my thoughts of Tia.

My sister Tempest is nineteen years old and studying Archaeology in college. It seems we both have a knack for the study of old things. I have a Master and PhD in Art History, and she is following in my footsteps in her own way. My parents gave her the name Tempest because even as a baby her emotions controlled the weather and as she got older her manipulation of it got stronger. I always envied my little sister for her control of her magic. Even at an early age, it just all flowed naturally. Maybe that is why my mother kept her close and encouraged me to go out and get a career and focus on being 'normal'. Well, I take that back not normal per se, that was my choice to just put my erratic magic on the back burner, I guess she wanted me to live within my limits. Who knows, maybe my mother was so protective of Tempest because she thought it would be her instead of me?

"Thanks sis," I say to her. She walks past Xavier handing him the clothes and they both walk over to the bed.

"I am going to have a shower while you two catch up," Xavier says as he leans over and kisses my forehead. "Thanks for the clothes, Tempest," he says as he walks through the bathroom door and closes it behind him.

"So, how does it feel to know you are marrying a half angel-half human hybrid?" She pushes me over and sits next to me on the bed.

"I don't know really. I guess I haven't had a chance to really process it, any of it." The way things are going, I don't think I will ever get that opportunity. I am literally hitting the ground running.

"Tempest, Shade is in my head. I heard him after I left the great room this morning. I don't know how I am going to get out of this deal, but I must. I can't go to the Underworld. I can't leave you all." I am panicking by the time I get to the end of what I'm saying to her. Yesterday I was just a witch with some crazy ass magic curating art for a living. Now I don't know what I am, and I feel as if my world has turned upside down.

"Nev, we are all going to work it out, we are in this together. Kes and I have been looking through some of the elder's diaries and we think we know why the angels got involved," she says with such hope I can't do anything but smile at her enthusiasm. I want to believe it will be ok and at the end of the week this will all be like a bad dream.

"We believe Great uncle Thomas spoke to the angels before he passed away. But before I get into that, get dressed and come down for lunch/dinner." She hugs me tight and pulls away with a knowing smile. "Bra and panties," she laughs and lifts her eyebrows suggestively at me.

"Hey, he slept on top of the covers, thank you very much. Last time I checked; I am a grown ass woman." I laugh and throw a pillow at her. She walks out the door and turns toward me.

"As far as Shade reaching out to you telepathically, that is something we are going to have to talk to mom about. So just ready yourself for that this evening. I know that you both bump heads and this morning was very amusing to watch, but I think you two need to have a real serious talk. Love ya, Sis." I hear her say as she closes the door behind her.

"Love you too," I yell back, jumping out of bed and grabbing the clothes my sister bought me. "Yoga pants and long t-shirt for the win," I say to myself and smile. She knows me so well. Hey, it's a staple.

Thinking about what Tempest said, I can't say I don't agree with my mother, and I need to clear the air and have a serious discussion about everything that has happened. I need her more than I care to admit, and I need all the help I can get. So, if I need to apologize for this morning, I will. I will play the role she wants me to play whilst getting the answers I need at the same time.

Hearing the shower still going, I wonder if Xavier will let me join him. Hey, kill two birds with one stone, right?

14

NEV

"Do you think the angels will make an appearance soon? I would really like to talk to them about the discussion that they had with Great uncle Thomas," I say to Xavier as we make our way to the kitchen in search of food.

"I am sure I will hear from my father soon. When he told me you were in danger, I demanded he no longer left me in the dark and that I needed answers. Hopefully, Tempest will be able to tell us what she and Kes read about in your uncle's diary that you mentioned."

"Can't you just call his name, and he will come?" I asked, completely clueless in the whole angel summoning protocol. I thought they were always listening out for humanity's call. I am sure Raphael will answer his son's call. Right?

"I can try after we speak to your mother. Or we can split up?" He looks down at me as I stop short of the kitchen door. I want to say yes, because we can get a lot done if we each take a parent and get the information we need. But I don't want to be apart from him any longer than I need to. I guess subconsciously I am counting down the days until I am snatched from his life. So, now I am clinging to him for as long as I can. *Give up much, Nev.* I berate myself. I am stronger than this and I will not do the whole damsel in distress routine. Looking up at Xavier, I reach out and grab his hand.

"Yes, let's split up and we can report back our findings."

We are greeted by most of the family as I walk through the kitchen door, pulling him along behind me.

Everyone is tucking into the buffet style dinner the kitchen staff have put on for us this evening. Considering how many of us are staying at the manor, I expect all food will be served this way from here on out. Well, at least until this is over. The poor cooks aren't accustomed to there being so many of us under one roof, except for the holidays of course. Who knows how long we will all be made to stay here? *Six more days Neveah,* I recall Shade's voice in my head and shudder. I have yet to tell Xavier that he can reach me through telepathy, and I need to. I need to shield my mind from him somehow.

"Nev, get a plate we've saved you and Xavier a seat at the table," Siobhan shouts to me from across the room.

I grab a plate; my stomach begins to growl at what I see before me. On the huge island in the middle of the kitchen there are trays of fried chicken, fries, and buttermilk biscuits. I look over to where my aunt is filling her plate with macaroni and cheese, collard greens, and to the left is a gigantic bowl of jambalaya. I can hear Xavier laughing at me as I rush over and start scooping up spoonsful for myself.

"Hey, save some for me now." my Aunt Daria says as she laughs and hip bumps me gently.

Everyone is laughing and mingling and enjoying each other's company and I forgot how the comradery of family makes you feel so much joy. I take it all in and hold this moment in my heart to remind me that I am alive and present.

Plate piled high with food, I make my way over to my cousins and take a seat next to Tia, who is devouring a plate of shrimp scampi. If dinner is like this every night none of us are going to be able to fit out the door. I have a wedding dress to get into in a few days, but I don't regret my food choices one bit. Xavier sits across from me next to Siobhan and Eddy. Kes, Tempest, and my Tamara all sit around the table near us, and all eyes are on me as I enjoy my food.

"I think they are all waiting for you to start spilling." Tia nudges me with her elbow.

"You might want to come up for air eventually, Nev," my sister says and laughs.

"I haven't had anything to eat since I left work yesterday. Hey, we don't get food like this every day, I was just enjoying it before I start talking and can't eat any more," I tell them all.

Pushing my plate away, I look at them and tell them everything.

∽

"White flames?"

"I can't believe you took out an entire horde of Shadow demons. That's some serious juice you're packing."

"So, how long has your magic being going erratic?"

"You say he is talking to you telepathically?"

I am tackling each question one at a time as they bombard me one after the other. I honestly should have come with a leaflet so that I could just hand out all the information needed, then I wouldn't have to repeat myself.

"I wonder what the underworld is like?" Eddy muses.

We all look at her as if she has sprouted horns. I mean to be honest with myself in the past few hours I have asked the same question. If I had no choice, could I spend the rest of my life in the underworld? The only thing I can picture is fire and brimstone, and heat so unbearable you can't breathe. I hate being hot. Ugh.

"What kind of question is that Eddy?" Tia spits back at her.

"Look maybe Nev needs to be realistic here, maybe this is the shit we need to be talking about." Eddy makes her point by stamping her finger on the dinner room table. “Maybe she needs to accept her fate, haven’t we all.”

“Maybe you have Eddy, but you talk as if Neveah should be tossed away like trash. She is an Owensen, yes, we were born into a situation none of us chose, but why should we have to just fall in line when it is obvious something nefarious going on.” I look over at Siobhan and I nod my head in agreement. I can’t help but think about what Eddy is saying and a part of me understands it. She’s tired. Hell, we all are. But I am not offering myself up as a sacrifice for some shady ass deal. I can’t, and I won’t accept it.

“It’s apparent that Lucifer, I mean ‘Shade,’” Kes air quotes, “has an agenda and he moved our family around like pieces on a chessboard.”

“Which brings us back to Great Uncle Thomas and the Archangel?” My sister Tempest silences the table, and they all look to Xavier as if he has all the answers.

“You know just about as much as I do now ladies. He shrugs. I am going to call on my father and see if he can be a bit more forthcoming about the events that have led us all here. I can’t guarantee he will reveal much, but I do think that if anything they need to speak with Neveah.” I grab his hand and gently squeeze it under that table.

“So, what did the diary say Tempest?” Looking between her and Kes, I can tell they have been eager to share. Kes grabs the book that’s been sitting between her and my sister and flips a few pages.

“We can tell by the number of diaries that Thomas kept that he wrote about the family's life after the deal in great detail. He talks about his mother’s frustrations and how she felt like she had no choice but to make the deal to save our sacred family land. He talks about the rift it created between his parents and how eventually his father and mother were married in name only. He gave up on loving her, never truly forgiving her for the consequences making that deal had on our family. But that was just me skimming through a few diaries he had written in his early twenties." Tempest shrugs. "The interesting stuff comes years later." She looks over at Kes as if giving her the go ahead to read it out loud to us.

May 1, 1995

It seems clear to me now that my days on this earth are numbered. I can feel the heavenly Father calling me home, but there is much more I must do to make sure that I can protect our family even in death. All the planning my mother put in place to keep the family safe is just not enough. Over the years, it became painfully clear that no more male children were being born, and my shifting abilities have now been passed on to my own daughters and granddaughters. I was truly the last male born to my family, and Lucifer made good on what he promised and what he would take away. Our family is respected and has thrived these past 75 years, and we leave our magical legacy to our future children. The Owensen name all but dies with me. As the women marry, they must keep their name instead of taking their husbands. The men who marry into this family, unfortunately, I feel, are the cursed ones. Never truly a part of the family and never the heads of their own households. The last of us males are far too old and have passed on to do much more than watch as we pair off the girls so that they can protect each other—shifters with their elemental sister counterparts. I am not sure how accurate this is, but it appears that after one of the women is married off and starts a family, we deem it safe for them to live a normal life. How true this is; we just don't know? Lucifer has not returned to claim any of the daughters so far, but we know he is watching. So, what I'm about to do now, is to protect our future. I will beg the heavenly Father to hear my prayers and send us a way to break this deal that has plagued our family for so long. I will return to the woods and kneel in supplication in the light of day, and I will pray without ceasing until I am heard. Every secret wish is a prayer the bible tells us.

"Wow, I was just ten at the time of that entry." I hear Eddy say softly to herself. I think we are all stunned by all that we heard. Looking over at Xavier, I can see the wheels turning for him as well.

"What do you think of all this?" I lean in and whisper to him. Wondering if he is going to say something profound about it all. I don't know where Kes and Tempest dug this up from, but none of us around this table were ever privy to any of this information. This family should be an open book regarding our situation, but instead all the elders have chosen to be tight-lipped about everything. As much as I would like Kes to read more I think it is time for me to find my mother.

"I was thinking about how old I was when he wrote that entry into his diary."

"What, were you like ten years old?" I try to do the math in my head.

"No, more like one-hundred-and-twenty-five."

Did he just say that he was one-hundred-and-twenty-five in the year 1995? Wait, that makes Xavier one-hundred-and-fifty-years old. My fiancée is *one-hundred-and-fifty-years old.*

"I have lived a long-life Neveah." I know everyone heard what he told me by the look of shock on their faces.

"It doesn't change who he is to you, Nev," Siobhan says as if reading my thoughts. She is right about that. I love Xavier, old man and all.

"No more surprises, right?" Oh please, let that be all.

"Right," he says and kisses me.

"Neveah, your mother would like to have a word in private," My dad says as he approaches us.

Well, I guess it's time to snatch the band aid right off.

15

NEV

"Hi, dad." I hug my father tight and take a moment to breathe and prepare myself for what's coming. It's been a few months since I have physically seen my dad and just being in his presence grounds me. Leaning back and looking him in his eyes, I wonder if he is an angel as well? I notice he has the same effect on me as Xavier now that I can sense his powers. I wonder.

"Hey dad, if you were an angel, you would tell me, right?"

"Oh, Neveah, we all have our secrets." He winks and walks off down the hallway leading to my mother's study.

"Wait, dad, seriously." I stare at his back as he walks away and then hurry to catch up.

"You know I am joking." He smiles. "But speaking of angels, I just want you to know that I was kept in the dark about Xavier too." Looking up, I can see the clench of his jaw and the thinning out of his lips, and I know that he was not pleased with my mother.

"Well, he's still Xavier, just with superpowers. Oh, and by

the way, he's one-hundred-and-fifty-years old. I just found out that little tidbit before you came to get me."

"Really?" He stops for a second as if he is processing what I just said and then continues. "I guess one-hundred-and-fifty years is kind of like thirty-five years in the life of a Nephilim. Your mother did tell me that they live for a very long time earlier this morning. I guess I didn't question how old Xavier was. Guess you're right, Xavier is still Xavier."

"Yes, he is." I follow my dad through the labyrinth of hallways of the main house. We make small talk about my mother and aunts and, lastly, renovations to the grounds and the individual wings of the manor. I wasn't surprised that my mother took it upon herself to claim her own study while my aunts shared the other a few doors down.

Walking through the study door, I see that my mother is standing with her back to us and lifts her finger as she finishes off her phone call. I look around the vast room lined with ancient text, grimoires, diaries of family members, spell books, and enchanted items. It's like a supernatural Smithsonian in here with all the items on display, from ancient totems. These carved wood figurines represent the spirit animals of our shifters, and wait, that's actual teeth. I quickly walk away from the display case until I notice a book on demons of the Underworld on my mother's desk. Glancing back at my father, who has taken a seat in one of the many comfy chairs around the room, I cross to him and sit down while we wait.

"Guess she's doing some light reading," I whisper as I relay the book I saw on her desk.

"Yes, she hasn't stopped looking at that book since the moment Tia sent out the alert last night," he says with a sigh.

On this, my mother and I agree. I want to know exactly what's out there and who's coming for me. Judging by the shadow demon attack last night, I think that was just a starter. In fact, by the things that Shade said to me this morning, I bet it's a guarantee.

"I can assure you, Meridith, that with all of our enchantments and shields in place that everyone will be safe for Friday's wedding. Please tell the council to alert all the necessary families and extend a last-minute invitation. Yes, I will let her know. Goodbye." Hanging up her phone and turning around, my mother sits properly at her desk and looks at dad and me as if we are just another tick on her agenda for the day.

"Did you sleep well, Neveah? I really do hope so because that tantrum this morning was beneath you," she says as she continues to busy herself tidying her desk.

"I did, but if you are expecting me to apologize, I am sorry, but I can't." Way to go back on your word Nev, I think to myself. But she lost me at tantrum, and I'll be damned if I apologize for telling the truth. Leaning forward and placing my hands on my knees, I take a calming breath. My father, who is still silent next to me, just reaches over and puts a comforting hand on my back. I look over, give him a slight smile, then force myself to focus back on my mother.

"So, since we are not going to get anywhere regarding this morning, daughter, I wanted to let you know that you have your final dress fitting tomorrow." She picks up her phone and scrolls through her list as if there is absolutely nothing wrong at all.

"You and Xavier need to approve the final menu, and since we have cut three weeks off this wedding planning, most of the wedding team will be in the guesthouses and starting their set up on Wednesday." She finishes and looks up at me, waiting for me to roll over, heel, or beg for a treat. I am completely gob-smacked.

"I didn't come here to talk about wedding plans. I didn't come in here to talk about cake, dresses, caterers, or any of that shit. Excuse my French, but you have completely lost it, Mother. If you think any of that means anything to me right now, then you don't know me at all." I stand and mouth a sorry to my dad and start pacing.

"Tia and I almost didn't make it here last night. I demolished a crap ton of shadow demons and the surrounding forest with magic I didn't know I had. I just found out my fiancée is a

Nephelium, and his father is the Archangel Raphael. I can hear Lucifer, wait I correct myself, Shade, speaking to me in my head, telling me that my fate is inevitable. But no, please continue to talk to me about how you, for the fiftieth time, don't approve of my dress choice or that you prefer white roses to the purple orchids I chose." By the time I finish, I am furious, and I feel tingling throughout my body. I feel as if I am on fire and look back at my dad, who jumps up and gathers me up in his arms. I am trying so hard to control whatever is happening to me and not hurt him at the same time. I feel as if my skin is rippling, and a shooting pain spears me between my shoulder blades, and I know that something is wrong. I have never felt pain like this before. I angle my hands away from my father as my fire magic is going out of control, reacting to everything I am feeling, yet I have no control. I can't hear what's happening around me as my father gently lowers me to the floor due to the spike in my heart rate pounding my eardrums. I can feel feet moving and furniture scrapping along with the hardwood floors from whoever has entered the room. The pain is taking me under, and I try to open my eyes to see everyone around me, but the light is so blinding I squeeze them shut again. I don't know what's happening to me, and for the first time in a long time, I am scared.

The last thing I hear before the lights go out is my father calling my mother's name.

"Willa!"

16

TIA

I knew something was wrong. I could feel it in my gut. My intuition never fails when it comes to my sister witch. I can always tell when something isn't right, but this feels completely different, and I have the strongest urge to get up and find her. I look up as I rub at my chest because my spirit animal can feel it too and she is about ready to break free and fly us out of the room.

"What's up Tia?" My sister asks, sensing my unease they all turn their attention my way.

"Something is up with Nev." I push back my chair and run through the main house in search of her.

"She's in mom's study," I hear Tempest say as she and Kes are right behind me.

I can almost feel her pain and I pick up the pace as I turn down the hallway. Why does this place have to be so damn big? I know we have a large family, but it makes getting somewhere in a hurry such a chore. Feeling frustrated because I can't remember which study belongs to whom anymore, I stop and let Tempest take the lead.

I hear Siobhan behind us, but at a distance, and I shout at her to go and get Xavier. The last thing he would want is to know Nev was in trouble and not be here with her. Another faint wave of pain hits me, but I continue after Tempest and Kes toward the study.

Running into the room, we all stop short at the scene in front of us.

Uncle Gavin is barely holding Nev up with her arm stretched wide away from them both as little bursts of fire shoot out and hover over her fingertips. Nev's head is back, and her eyes are so white they look as if they are glowing, her mouth open in a silent scream. The most bizarre sight of all is the outstretched wing that is protruding from the left side of her body. If I wasn't so shocked, I could have admired the brown and black iridescent wing that stretched all the way to my aunt's desk, knocking over everything in its path to freedom.

"We need to get her on the floor," my uncle says to us, and we spring into action. I start moving chairs and tables while Tempest and Kes started rolling back the Persian rug on the floor. All I want to do is get to Nev, so with the last chair back against the bookshelf, I rush over to help ease her to the floor.

"Nev, can you hear me?" I say to her, but from the way she is squeezing her eyes shut and the faint pain I can feel, I know she is lost to us right now.

"What do we—" Is all I get out before I'm flying across the room toward the door and sliding into the hallway. I don't even register the pain I am feeling and jump up and run back into the room. Again, I am shocked by the scene in front of me, in the exact place where I was kneeling on the floor is Nev's other wing that had shot out of her right shoulder blade and sent me airborne into the hall.

I look up at my aunt, who is staring in disbelief at what has taken in place in her study. Tempest and Kes are trying to gently bring Nev's wings in toward her body, but those bad boys ain't having none of it. I can see Nev's eyes trying to open, but as soon as she looks toward me, she goes limp in my uncle's arms.

Uncle Gavin looks up and yells my Aunt Willa's name to snap her into action. "Willa."

My aunt rounds her desk and kneels at Nev's head, placing her hands on either side. As she closes her eyes and chants softly, I can hear feet running down the hall.

"Is she ok?" Siobhan stops beside me and looks over my shoulder into the room.

"Holy shit," is all she gets out before Xavier and a man with the huge white wings materialize right before our eyes.

"Holy shit indeed."

17

XAVIER

I made my excuses to the ladies and made my way back to Neveah's room in search of a quiet place to reach out to my father. It is not often that I call on him, I usually just rely on him reaching out to me when he needs me. After the events of the last few hours, I think it's time for me to hear the whole story and get any information that can help Neveah as I can. I thought things would be a little strain now that everyone knew what I was, but everyone was just as welcoming and eager to feed me as they always were. Thank the heavens for that, because all I can think is that I don't want to make things more stressful than they already are.

Making my way into her room, I smile at the memory of her waking up in my arms this afternoon. I take comfort in knowing that in a few days she will be my wife and we will have so many mornings to look forward to. We both made a promise to wait until we were married after I proposed to her, but now with everything hanging in the balance, the need to be with her weighs heavy in my heart. We are by no means innocent, but I am a gentleman first and foremost. I walk out to the balcony, lean against the rail and stare out into the evening sunset. The sky around the manor sparkles with enchantments. This place is so heavily guarded, who knows what is happening just on the other side. I only hope and pray that it is enough.

I close my eyes and empty my mind of all thoughts and speak to the wind.

“Father if you can hear me—"

“Xavier, son I can always hear you.” My father’s feet touch the balcony floor, and he joins me at the rail.

I shake my head and smile. That didn’t take as much effort as I thought. I think about all the times I wanted to reach out and never did. Always thinking about my place and where I stood in the “angelic hierarchy”, that I didn’t deem it appropriate to just call on my father like a child would. Yes, he is my father, but my mother always told me that he had an important job to do, and we were blessed to be in his presence. I took whatever moments I could when I could get them and nothing more.

“Father thank you for coming,” I say to him, because I am truly thankful for him showing up so quickly. I thought I would be at this for some time.

“I know what you want to discuss my son and I am ready to answer your questions. We are at a crucial moment and there is no more need for discretion.” He raises his head to the heavens as if hearing someone speak to him and shakes his head.

“Ask.”

“What did Nev’s Uncle Thomas ask of the Archangels? Why did Shade choose Neveah? How can we stop him from taking her?” I ask in quick succession.

“Close your eyes my son and see what I see.” He grabs my hand and I close my eyes. Suddenly we are standing in the forest on the grounds of the manor.

“This is the memory of the day in which Thomas came down to the forest to pray for help for his family.” That was all he said before Nev’s uncle Thomas walked slowly into the clearing and fell to his knees and prayed out loud.

Saint Michael the Archangel,

defend us in battle,

be our protection against the wickedness and snares of the devil.

May God rebuke him, we humbly pray,

and do thou, O Prince of the heavenly host,

by the power of God, cast into hell.

Satan and all the evil spirits

who prowl through the world seeking the ruin of souls.

Amen.

My family has been made a pawn in Lucifer's games, Father God, he has taken what is most precious and taken advantage of the gift that you bestowed upon our family. I ask you to send your angels down to help us. For the future of my family is beyond my sight and I fear for what's to come.

With his head bowed and his arms outstretched to the sky he prays until the sun begins to set and I know that his time is almost up. If you want the light to hear you, you must pray in the light. Looking at Neveah's uncle, I could see the toll that kneeling was taking on his aged body, but he did not move, and he continued to pray so softly that I could not hear what he was saying.

I turn to my father to ask him what happened, but instead I turned my face up to the sky as two bright lights descended to the ground and hovered just above Thomas's bowed head. One of them touched down to earth and walked silently around Thomas, looking out amongst the trees as if surveying the land. His wings shone as bright as the sun, and his hair cascaded down his back in silver ringlets. He wore a metal breastplate to cover his cream-colored tunic and trousers. But the most striking of all, were the two-flaming swords strapped across his back. He was tall, strong, and formidable, but he radiated peace and tranquility at the same time. Archangel Michael. Turning back to his angelic counterpart, he gives a quick nod and the other angel lands gracefully to the ground.

"Gabriel," my father says to me as we continue to watch the

scene. I have met Michael on several occasions, but I never crossed paths with God's Messenger. He was not as tall as Michael and had the brightest green eyes that looked as if they could see straight through you. He had golden wings and a horn strapped to his waist that swayed gently as he walked over to Thomas.

"Thomas, son of Magnolia, we have heard your prayers," Michael says as he touches Thomas's shoulder.

Thomas supplicates more, leans down and places his head to the grounds as if he didn't dare look at them.

"Rise Thomas, son of Magnolia, we have come to tell you of many things to come," Gabriel says as he helps Thomas up from the ground.

"We are here to help."

We listened then to what the angels told Thomas about the legacy of the Owensen family, and how Lucifer in his haste did not hear the entire prophecy he overheard the Shaman speak of in the flames that night hundreds of years ago. They spoke of a witch who would bring a balance to light and dark, that she would be "God's Left Hand" here on earth. They said that she would be the wielder of the righteous flame and blot out the darkness that plagued mankind. They spoke of a time when Lucifer could no longer come back to earth and would be trapped in the Underworld for all eternity, but a battle would have to be won and only she could do this deed.

"When the time comes, we will visit the child and bestow on her God's gifts, but they will only manifest themselves if she is chosen by Lucifer to be his bride," Michael says to Thomas.

"He will not be able to resist such a strong pull of magic. He will choose the right witch when the time comes Thomas," Gabriel reassures Thomas, answering my question before I could voice what I was wondering as well. What if Lucifer chose the wrong Owensen witch?

I know Neveah is who the archangels foretold, and now I must consider what this means for our future. How do I protect someone who eventually will not need my protection? I love Neveah and I will be whatever she needs me to be, but once she knows who she is and what she is meant to do, will my love be enough? All these questions are bombarding me as I look at the scene before me.

"Will my family ever have male children again?" Thomas asks Gabriel.

"Yes, there will be male shifters in your family again. A female of your family will conceive in or around the time the hand is chosen. Thomas, your family's sacrifice has not gone unnoticed, and we all know the lengths Lucifer went through to use your family for his own gains."

"Now, we wait. When the time comes, we will make sure she understands her destiny," Michael says.

Just as he was about to say more, I hear a loud bang and my father, and I are back standing on the balcony. To be honest, I think that we've been standing here the whole time and what I saw was just a vision.

"Xavier!!" Siobhan yells as she crosses the room and stops short when she sees my father.

"Who—" I cut her off before she can start asking questions.

"What's wrong, Siobhan?" I ask, sensing her distress.

"It's Nev, something's wrong and she needs you. Meet everyone in my aunts' study," she says as she turns and runs out the room.

"She is transitioning. We must get to her; I do not know the extent of her magic or what gifts she has been given. For the first time in a very long time, I will be just as surprised as you are," my father says before I can ask. Placing his hand on my shoulder, we both appear suddenly in the middle of Neveah's mother's study.

"Holy shit," Siobhan says as she stands behind Tia at the door.

"Everyone, stand back," my father commands as he walks over to Neveah and places his finger on her forehead. She goes completely still. Everyone looks on in shock as he lifts her in his arms and her wings retreat into her body.

"She will need rest. Once she is awake, there will be much to discuss," he says to the room as he places Neveah in my arms.

Looking down at the love of my life, I hold her close and vanish.

18

NEV

Well, I know for sure that I am not in my mother's office anymore. I take stock of my body and the pain that radiated through me before I blacked out is gone. I feel amazing. I'm engulfed in fluffy pillows and my nice warm duvet, so I gather I am back in my room. The last thing I remember before I went under was the excruciating pain in my shoulder blades and back. Did I shift? If so, I didn't get to meet my spirit animal. I don't feel any different. Tia told me she could feel her spirit animal just underneath her skin, always there, ready and waiting. Nope, not spirit animal then. I could hear people in the room, but I didn't want to open my eyes yet. I have no clue what happened to me back there. I was so angry with my mother's callus treatment of our current situation that I guess I just lost it. Time to wheel it in Neveah. I need to figure out what's happening to me and fast because time was getting away from me.

"Neveah, I have not been able to sense you for three days. Where have you been hiding, love? Have you learned to shield

your thoughts from me now? My, my, my, you are one clever girl indeed. So strong."

I had almost forgotten about my telepathic link to the devil himself. Wait, did he just say three days? There is no way I've been out for that long. What the hell happened? He can't hear me anymore, but I can still talk to him. Well, this may work in my favor.

"I have been right here, Shade. Yes, maybe I have learned a trick or two. But I think that's enough talking between you and me," I say with absolute conviction, so that he believes every word. I hope.

"Oh, Neveah, I was so worried I was about to cause some serious trouble and come in there and get you myself. I would hate to have to kill your entire family. Oh, and by the way, you only have three more days. Goodbye, for now." His laugh lingers as I feel him leave my mind.

I mentally put up a wall in hopes that I can do whatever I've been doing to block him from my mind. Damn it, *three days*, I better not waste any longer in this bed; I am sure there are several pairs of eyes waiting for me to wake.

I sit up and open my eyes. "I have been out for three days? What happened to me?" I guess it wasn't the slow and easy wake up they were expecting by the looks on their faces. All except Tia, who is laughing in the doorway of the room.

"Well, hello to you to sleeping beauty," she says and makes her way past a man standing in the center of the room, who I hadn't noticed until now. His grey robes and white wings scream angel, and I am in shock as I look at who I am assuming is Xavier's father, Raphael.

"Don't worry you're not going crazy he just appeared out of thin air," Tia says as she sits next to me on the bed, I know she wants to say more but waits patiently for him to speak.

"I am so glad you're awake," Xavier says as he stands from the armchair, I hope he hasn't been sleeping in and sits next to me on the bed, sandwiching me between him and Tia. My pillars of strength the two of them.

"Neveah, this is my father, Raphael," he says and grabs my hand and kisses it.

I look at him and instantly feel the wave of calm wash over me like the breeze on a warm summer's day. It's just nice. So, I guess it really is an angel thing.

"I am honored, sir." I mean, how do you address an Archangel?

"No, the honor is all mine Neveah. I am glad you have completed your transition and that I can help you in any way possible to prepare you for what's to come." He smiles softly and nods his head.

"Transition?" I am so confused right now. "Transition into what. Did I shift? I didn't think I had the shifter gene, but anything is possible in this family." I look to them all and wait for them to answer.

"Surely—"

"Oh, Neveah honey, you're awake. Oh, thank God." My mother rushes into the room with my father right behind her. Seeing there is no way she can get to me; she stands near the foot of the bed looking so worried and lost that I really don't know how to feel about it. My father rests his hands on her shoulders and gently pulls her away toward the wall where he wraps his arms around her for comfort. I don't think I have ever seen my mother look so distraught. I look at my father and the worry on his face fades away as he offers me a reassuring smile.

"So, transition?"

"There is so much to discuss and so little time to tell you all you need to know. I will tell you everything and then you can ask all the questions you need to," Raphael says.

And then he begins to tell a tale that would rival any fantasy novel I have ever read. A funny tale about a prophecy and being the chosen one who can harness the power of all the elements, summon a righteous flame, God's left hand, and that's not the most bizarre part of the story. Supposedly, I sprouted angel wings right before I blacked out in my mother's office.

Angel wings.
I guess I am with Tia on this one.
You can't make this shit up. Oops. Can I still say shit?
Damn.

19

NEV

"So, am I an angel now?"

"No, you are still human and a witch, but one of your gifts from heaven are your wings," Raphael says.

"I am God's left hand. My job is to defend the world from darkness. I am his justice on earth," I say to myself. I feel as if the rug has been snatched from under me. How? No, why would they put such a responsibility on the shoulders of one person. Why wasn't I prepared for this my entire life? I am twenty-five years old, and my magic feels as if I am sixteen again and just coming into my own. I'm a curator. Not a fighter.

Pull it together, Nev. The last thing I need is a panic attack. I might blow the roof off the manor. My mother would lose her mind.

Speaking of mother.

"Did you know this momma?" I look over at her as she hangs on to my father, as if her life depended on it.

She looks so eager to speak and steps forward, but it is Raphael who answers my question.

"For a long time, we thought that Willa would be the chosen

witch because of how strong she is magically. But as the years passed, and she married your father, we came to her and only told her that one of you could possibly be chosen. So, we blessed you and Tempest when you were born and kept an eye on you both."

"Please understand, Neveah, that I assumed it would be Tempest. That's why I keep her close because she is the youngest and needs my protection. Tia is so strong, I never worried about you. Yes, your magic was always so volatile. Maybe I should have figured that there is a possibility it's that way because you were more. I should have nurtured you more. I should have pushed you into training instead of pushing you into a life of normality. For that I am truly sorry," my mother says as tears roll down her face. Her honesty and sincerity send a wave of shock through me.

"This is all news to us all and we can talk further once Neveah is acclimated. Right now, Willa, this is not the time. Let her come to you." My father hugs her close and steers her toward the door. My mother just looks back once more and smiles, and I know that it's her way of letting me know she will be waiting.

"Well, let's keep it real here family. We all thought it would be Tempest." Tia nudges my side and laughs. Always trying to diffuse the situation and I am so grateful she is here.

I could spend days asking questions, but I know that I don't have the time to dissect every aspect of who I am, what I've become. I have already lost three days, and with the wedding only days away and my imminent show down there is no time like the present.

"Well, I guess it's time I learned to fly."

20

XAVIER

I am no wings expert by any means, so when my father told me I should be the one to help Neveah fly, I laughed all the down to the training grounds of the manor. Several family members had come down to watch Neveah, to witness all her new abilities, and she certainly was a sight to behold.

"She can now control both flames and call them separately." My father appears next to me and looks up into the air where Tia is in eagle form circling and dodging Nev's attacks.

"Yes, and she can call on all four elements as well. She just needs time to train and get use to this new level of power," I say to him.

"What is your dad saying?" I jump because I can hear her in my head.

"So, your telepathy is not just with Shade. You can reach out to me as well?" I ask her. I want to express my relief to her and tell her that I was concerned that the connection was one sided. But instead, I just smile up at her and marvel at how she has taken to this so fast.

"Well, her telepathic link is not just to Shade. She just spoke to me," I say to my father.

"Excellent news, indeed," he says as he expands his wings and takes off toward Neveah.

I watch as they maneuver themselves in the air, and my thoughts turn to the future. The moment I took Neveah back to her room when her wings first appeared, I wondered what my place would be in her life. With such responsibility on her shoulders and everything that she is expected to achieve, can I remain by her side whilst she puts her life in danger daily? It was much easier protecting her when she could be potentially chosen. But now; I fear our paths are split. I love her with all my heart, and I don't want to lose her to her destiny. I'd rather die by her side than live the rest of my life without her.

"You're spiraling, Xavier. Whatever this life throws at us, we can tackle it together," she says to me. I am really going to have to get used to her being able to read my thoughts.

"I didn't realize I was thinking about it that hard," I say to her.

I guess this is just another conversation to put a pin in and something we can work out later. In two days, I plan to marry her no matter what trouble comes our way.

To live as long as I have, I count myself blessed. To have someone as special as Neveah in my life is a gift I will treasure always. I look up as my father stops mid-flight and looks to the forest surrounding the manor and vanishes. I can almost feel Neveah's panic as she looks down at me with worry on her face. Tia climbs higher into the sky and her spirit animal let out a loud high-pitched squawk. I teleport to the edge of the tree line. I can see movement just beyond the trees as the late afternoon sun cast shadows, making it difficult to tell what is rushing at us so quickly. I can hear Neveah telling her family to get to the house as fast as they can, and I see Tempest run toward me with her hands outstretched, calling the wind. I am so distracted by everything going on around me that I barely get out of the way of the snarling giant of a beast trying to take me by surprise.

Hellhounds. Huge wolf like creatures with enormous black teeth, dripping with what looks like molted lava, black leathery skin that barely clings to their skeletal bodies, and a long-spiked tail. Just beneath their skin you can see the orange glow of fire waiting to engulf anything and anyone in their path. They all come stalking out from the forest surrounding the manor. I teleport beside Tempest, as they continue to walk slowly toward us. Looking around, I see Neveah is still up in the air trying to make sure everyone is out of harm's way. I don't know how they got past the wards and barriers, and I have a feeling that my father went to investigate.

"Xavier, get my sister out of here," Neveah shouts down to me.

"Stop micromanaging the situation Nev, we do this together," Tempest shouts back.

She's right. We need to do this together; they can easily overwhelm the entire manor burning everything to the ground. Just as I was about to say that they all charge at us. Siobhan and Kes are in their spirit animal form, but I think everyone is a bit cautious in their attack approach. I don't think any of us have ever seen a hellhound, let alone fought one.

"Water and wind are the only thing I can think of." Tempest turns and runs, putting some space between her and the beast running toward us.

"I heard her," Nev said.

I watch both Tempest and Neveah call on the wind around us. The hellhounds begin to get pushed back into the forest. The ones that have gotten closer to us dig their sharp nails into the ground, as if they can call upon their fire below us. The ground begins to quake. I feel the rumble beneath my feet, and I grab Tempest and teleport us further toward the manor as the ground crumbles below us, trying to swallow us whole. I watch as the shifters jump, and dodge broken craters of fire that are appearing all around us.

Kes' jaguar bounds over a crater, but a hellhound catches her mid-jump, and she is knocked sideways into the flames. I know if I teleport to her, I won't be able to help her unless she shifts back to human form. But I didn't get a chance to move before Tia's eagle swoops down with her large talons, grabs Kes by the haunches and picks her right up out of the side of the crater she was clinging to. Tia's eagle is flying so low due to the weight she is carrying, she doesn't see the hellhound running toward her.

"Tia," Neveah screams from the air as she rushes toward them. Neveah stops mid-flight and watches as the hellhound jumps and catches Tia by surprise, grabbing her wing. Tia's wing catches fire and she falls with Kes' jaguar to the ground. Kes' spirit animal instantly jumps in front of her sister in a protective stance to face off against the hellhounds approaching them.

"We need to get to them, Xavier." Tempest grabs my hand and I teleport us right next to Tia's now naked body. I can see that her right arm is badly burned from her shoulder all the way down to her hand. But there is no time to attend to her as more hellhounds run toward us. We are surrounded and I am without a weapon to help Kes and Tempest. I look around and see shifters and witches using all their affinities to push the hellhounds back, but it doesn't seem to be working. So many are wounded, and I don't think we can keep this up much longer. I look up and see Neveah's arms outstretched, her eyes are a black void and from her hands she blasts the hellhound coming at us with ice. The hound freezes in its tracks.

"She just froze it," Tempest shouts over all the chaos around us.

I hear her, but my focus is still on Neveah who looks as if she has been possessed as she flies from hound to hound freezing them in action like statues.

"Do you think you can do the same?" I ask Tempest.

"Are you kidding me? I've never seen anyone do anything like that before. But I can keep them cold." Tempest stretches her arms to sky and freezing rain begins to fall from the sky. I bend down and gently scoop an unconscious Tia into my arms and hold her close to my body to keep her as warm as I can. No longer in danger, Kes runs off toward a small witch laying not too far from us. I can't tell who it is, but Kes shifts, lifts the girl into her arms and begins to run back to the manor.

"Xavier, get the wounded back to the manor." My father appears next to me as several armored angels appear out of the sky with flaming swords, aiming for all the frozen hellhounds. I watch as the angels strike the frozen beasts, shattering their bodies. All around us, the pieces of the hellhounds begin to melt and absorb into the ground.

"Get Tia back to the house, son. I will make sure Neveah is ok."

I am torn between leaving Neveah behind, but I glance up at her once more and I know she will be fine. I look down at Tia and teleport us back to the manor.

21

NEV

I feel out of control of my body as I fly through the surrounding forest, hunting down the last of the hellhounds and freezing them so the angels can finish the job. I watched that beast grab Tia out of the air and I don't remember anything after that; it was like I was on autopilot and my magic just took over. I guess I can add freezing creepy ass hellhounds to my list of new magic. I only woke up a few hours ago from my "transition sleep" and now I'm in full battle mode. I mean, can a sistah get a break? Just to get acquainted with all this newness before I go all Gandalf on everything around me. Some of the angels have caught up to me, so I decide to leave them to handle the rest. I thought flying with Raphael was amazing, but I am literally flying amongst angels in full battle armor with huge flaming swords. One stops in front of me and inclines his head in respect, I smile and nod back at him as he flaps his wings and takes off further into the forest. Out of the corner of my eye, I can see a huge black bear running through the forest toward the manor. I instantly know it's Eddy, she's a bit further into the forest than I would expect, but maybe she chased a hellhound all this way. I fly after her and make my way back to toward the manor. There are so many injured around me, and I know Xavier will be worried until he physically puts his hands on me.

"*I'm on my way to you,*" I speak to him telepathically. I don't know if I am ever going to get used to using my newly developed telepathy. I really thought it was something Shade was forcing on me; I had no idea I was already in pre-transition. Hey, I am still getting used to the idea that I can fly. I have wings. Reaching the clearing of the back of the manor, it is looks like a bomb has been detonated. All the shifters and witches who had been left injured are now back in the manor, and what is left is hard to look at. Huge, gaping, steaming holes in the ground, with fallen trees and training ground debris everywhere. They came into our home and tried to cause harm to my family. There was no reason for this attack. No reason other than Shade trying to grab me early and kill some of my family members for sport. Haven't we sacrificed enough? None of us were ready for what stalked through that forest, and we are going to have to get it together if something else decides to attack us.

"It's not like I am resisting," I say to myself. I will go when the time comes if I need to. I will not be the cause for any more harm to befall my family. Is this my fault? Should I have gotten out the car last Friday and just gone willingly with Shade? We all knew that this day would come and one of us would have to go with him. I am so angry I want to walk out beyond the barrier and face him down, make him pay for this. I know it was Shade, how he got past the wards I have no clue, but we need to find a way to keep the dregs of hell out. I see Xavier's father speaking with an angel with beautiful long silver hair and bright golden wings. What catches my eye the most is the doublè swords strapped to his back, and I remember what Xavier told me of his father's vision. I know he is the Archangel Michael.

"Neveah," Raphael calls me over and I land and walk over to them. I can feel Michael's eyes on me as I approach. I know when I am being sized up and the way he is looking at me right now, I begin to feel self-conscious. Maybe I am just imagining it.

"Raphael, and you are Michael" I say to them both. I extend my hand toward him, and he just looks down at it like I am offering him poison. Ok, I am not imagining it. Do angels shake hands? I need to ask Xavier for a quick lesson in angel etiquette. I am failing, apparently.

"Chosen," is all he says as he briefly inclines his head toward me and turns his attention back to Raphael. Well, that was rude. I didn't know angels could be rude, but Shade was once an angel, so maybe they walk a fine line like us mere mortals. I am not liking the fact that he is disregarding me at all. I didn't just fight off hellhounds to be disrespected by an archangel.

"Neveah," I say to him, and he glances at me once more. I can see a slight smile form on Raphael's face, but it's gone as soon as I blink, and I turn my attention to Michael. Yes, Raphael, I will not be walked over and I'm not a pushover. I will try a different tactic.

"Thank you for coming to the aid of my family." Let me just kill him with a little gratitude and see if he warms to me. I follow that with my award-winning smile just to put a cherry on top.

"It is our duty and nothing more. We don't interfere in human affairs, but you are an exception Neveah. Eventually you will manage without our help. You have a lot to learn and no time at all to learn it all. Your new abilities are impressive, but you are not ready to face Lucifer."

"Shade?" Why I feel the need to annoy him by correcting him. I know who Shade really is.

"Shade *is* Lucifer child. He picks a new name and decides to reinvent himself. He is just Lucifer to me."

Why does he annoy me so much? First impressions are everything and from the moment he looked at me like I was gum on his nicely cobbled leather sandal, I knew he and I were going to be a problem.

"You need a sword, and you need training."

"A sword? Are you kidding me? I have never even fired a gun, so I am not going to carry around a sword," I say to them both.

"You can't rely on your magic alone, Neveah," Raphael says to me.

"You both know that I have a wedding a day after tomorrow, right? I just learned to fly and use my magic at the same time barely an hour ago. Now you're telling me I need to learn to use a sword as well. Look, this is all just a little too much for me to handle right now. I will let you continue your conversation, and we can stick a pin in this for the moment," I say to them as I turn around to leave.

"I don't think there will be a wedding, Neveah," Raphael says to me. I stop in my departure and turn back to them.

"What are you saying?" My mother is determined to marry me to Xavier, as if that will change anything. But I will go through the motions and marry the man I love, even if I must walk away from him, eventually.

"I think you should return to the manor and check in with your family," Michael says to me. I quickly look to Raphael for an explanation, but he just hangs his head. Can they sense something I can't? Something is wrong. I reach out to Xavier and feel his anguish. I don't hesitate any longer. Extending my wings, I take off toward the manor as fast as my wobbly wings will carry me.

22

NEV

It looks like a battlefield triage hospital when I walk in through the front door of the manor. The foyer is full of family members running around attending to the wounded. As I walk through in search of Tia and Xavier, it appears that he has healed as many of my cousins as he can and only a few are still wearing bandages and slings. That's when I hear it. Someone is having a serious argument about something in the great room, I run down the hall and stand in front of chaos.

My Aunt Penny, the youngest of the elders, is holding her sixteen-year-old daughter Tamara in her arms and screaming at the top of her lungs. I can feel the pain and sorrow all over the room and I know that she is gone.

"You did this." My Aunt Joy points at Eddy, who is standing near the windows on the other side of the room. The room is completely silent for a moment, as everyone waits for what Eddy has to say. I just saw her come back from the woods and I know she would never do anything to hurt Tamara.

"I came out to fight just like every shifter here. I told Tamara to stay in the manor and not to follow me. I told her she is too young, and the enemy was unknown. None of us knew how to fight those things. None of us," she cries.

"I saw Eddy coming out of the wood after she had run down a hellhound just now. We were all outnumbered and lacking in how to fight those demons," I say to the room.

I look over to find Kes with an unconscious Tia in her arms as Xavier heals the burns all over her right arm. I walk over to them and ignore the wondering eyes that follow me across the room. My aunt was clutching to her child for dear life, rocking and sobbing, and I knew that if I went to her right now, there would be nothing I could say or do.

"Let the blame fall where it should go, shall we," my aunt Joy tells the room. She picks herself off the floor next to Tia and Kes and walks over to my mother who is standing next to the fireplace. There are so many of us in the room, I hadn't noticed that she was holding my Aunt Edina, who was crying silently on her shoulder.

"What are you implying, Joy?" she asks.

"We've been complacent and negligent of our duties as the elders of this family. We should have been teaching these girls about the enemy from the moment they were born. There were actual *hellhounds* in the backyard, and they had no clue. Hell, I had no clue. Did you, Willa? Oh, wait, you were trying to be a quick study and learn as much as you could on the fly. Yeah, I saw the book on the desk in your study the other day. *Your* study, like none of us are worthy enough to be in there but you. We are equal, yet you have believed yourself the ultimate decision maker. You would rather plan a wedding for a daughter who needed you, you should have been focused on her well-being this week, not a goddamn dress. Did you even see her out there? Your daughter has wings, Willa, she has all these new abilities. Just think of how easy it would have been for her to adjust if you would have spent as much time with her as you did Tempest. We have failed; therefore, we are responsible for that baby's death. Not Eddy, she was doing her duty and she is our strongest shifter. You couldn't possibly think she was supposed to stay behind and babysit." She is crying by the end of her rant. We are all crying by the end of everything she has said. The truth hurts. And my Aunt Joy had laid it on the table, bare for us all to see.

"I did what I thought was right. I thought that they didn't need to be battle ready. I didn't think any of this would happen this way. It's been so long and in every diary the duties passed down became less and less. I thought if I prepared them to live a normal life that I was doing what was best," my mother says to the room. I wanted to feel sad for her, but I just felt angry all over again. I had a feeling she wasn't talking to the room but to me directly. But I was not ready to deal with that yet.

"We need to be ready. Who knows if something else will try to come through the barriers?" Tempest says from the doorway with my father and uncles beside her. They all bring in Tamara's dad, who collapses next to his wife, and they cry silently together. My father glances around the room and finds me, and just from his look I know what needs to be said.

"We will talk about this later but understand this is for the best," I say to Xavier, and he only looks at me and nods.

"There will be no wedding," I say to my mother. "We will have a celebration in honor of Tamara to plan. That is what's most important now."

Of course, Tia picks that moment to jolt awake. Perfect timing, as usual.

"What did I miss?"

23

TIA

I am trying so hard not to blame myself. I think we all are, to be honest. We have always been taught to work in pairs to protect each other if we ever got into a situation where we had to fight. That was a rule in theory, not in practice. Everything was a theory, and we were so not prepared for that shit show outside. There was so much going on out there that you really couldn't focus on anything but keeping yourself out of harm's way. I knew Neveah would be ok because she was up in the air like I was. But watching all the other shifters struggle below was challenging for me to watch. It was the first time I ever felt helpless as I saw everyone I loved and cared about getting injured left and right. There was actual lava dripping from the hellhound's teeth. It was an experience that I never want to have to go through again, and when I saw my sister fall between that massive crater in the ground, I lost it. I have never pushed my spirit animal before, and we have never had to haul something so heavy. Kes as a jaguar weighs a ton, and I'd be damned if I lost her to the fire, so of course, I wasn't flying high enough when that asshole of a hound clipped my wing. Talk about hurt like hell; I passed out and shifted as soon as we hit the ground.

Thank goodness for angels and their healing power because that would have taken a while for me to recover from. But even with all that going on, I hadn't noticed Tamara out on the field, and I hadn't noticed Eddy either. I guess Nev was right, and she was chasing them off through the trees. With all the chaos, I don't think anyone took stock of the children and younger witches in the manor, and that is something else that needs to change. I didn't hear my mother's rant being passed out and all, but from what Nev and Kes told me later, I would have backed her 100%. Hey, I am all for this place becoming a mini-Hogwarts if it means we know exactly what we are up against the next time it happens because I know that this will happen again. I don't want Neveah to go with Shade, and I am not the only person in this family who thinks it. If we must fight to keep her here, then I feel we should do just that. We have never lost a family member like this before, Tamara died attempting to protect our family and home, and she deserved a proper send-off today. We spent the day before canceling wedding plans and preparing for my little cousin's funeral. So, of course, I am stalling because the last thing I want to do is face this day. Nev's time was up, and one way or another, today is about more than just what we lost but what we could be losing. She is like a sister, and I must protect her and keep her safe, even though she doesn't really need me. We have no idea when Shade's going to come and collect, but I don't think Nev is just going to walk out of the barrier and present herself to him. This day will get messy and wearing white will really suck at the end of the day, but it is tradition for us to wear white instead of black. We wear white in celebration in the hope that our loved ones will be reborn again. We wear white for most of the family rituals and ceremonies, and as I look through the spare closet in my room, I finally find something decent to wear.

I cross over to the bed and lay my clothes out as I hear a knock at the door.

"Come in," I say to whoever it is. I have spent enough time with my own thoughts, and I need a distraction. To be honest, the last person I expected to walk through the door was Eddy. I feel for her, and I can't imagine what is going through her head now. She walks in with a sense of urgency, and I am a little shocked at how focused she looks right now. She sits on the ottoman at the end of the bed but then gets up again as if she will leave the room. I block her exit and place my hands on her shoulders, and she looks at me as if she remembers why she came in here and goes to sit back down.

"Are you ok, Eddy?" I ask her as I pull my hoodie over my head and begin to dress.

"Tia, we need to talk. I want to apologize for the way I have been acting the past few days. Truth be told, this has all been a shock to everyone's system, and I guess I got wrapped up in the idea of normality, you know?" she says to me as if I was going to agree.

"No, Eddy, I don't know. You were ready to throw Neveah to the wolves for what you call 'normality. You are not thinking straight, Eddy, and you haven't really been present lately. You are the best of us, and you are the example we are told to follow as shifters. It was you who told us to 'protect at all costs, 'our sister witch is our number one priority and most importantly, 'their life before our own. So no, I am not in a hurry for so-called normality. Hell, no one in this damn family knows what that is," I spit back at her.

"So, you blame me too. I told Tamara to stay indoors and do not come out until I came back for her. You know how willful she was, and she was so determined to prove herself that she disobeyed me and got herself killed. I will never forgive myself for losing her. But I told her not to leave. I had to go and do what I promised. I didn't have a choice."

I don't know if I know this woman sitting before me. Maybe it's grief and regret that has taken hold of her, but something is just not right here. Why did she sound so defeated? Resigned?

"What do you mean, promised Eddy?" I ask her. She looks at me in shock but covers it up quickly.

"The promise to do my duty, Tia, to our family. The promise we have all made," she says hastily.

"Look, I just came in here to apologize and clear the air with you. It's my turn to stand vigil over Tamara's body while Penny takes a break before the funeral. She was there all night as they washed, cleaned, and prayed over her in preparation for today." She gets up and quickly walks out the door.

"What just happened?" I say to myself.

I don't know what is wrong with Eddy, but something is not right.

24

NEV

We didn't get to speak all day really, separated and given our own tasks to help cancel our wedding and get ready for Tamara's funeral. I find it hard to even say her name in my head. I will never forget the sounds coming from my Aunt Penny as she held on to her baby girl. Baby, that was exactly what she was to all of us. She had just turned sixteen and was adjusting to her life with magic at her fingertips. She could manipulate and control water and was learning quickly with Tempest as her tutor and Eddy her guardian. Of course, she thought that she could help. I am just sorry that I hadn't noticed her running around out there. I thought I had made sure everyone who wasn't supposed to be there had gone inside. I quickly wipe a tear away at the sorrow I felt for the loss of someone so young.

"It's ok to cry," Xavier said to me as we lay face to face in my bed. With his eyes still closed, he reaches out and strokes my cheek and I lean into it for comfort. If I could stay right here in this moment and forget all about everything else this day would bring, I would.

"What can I say to you this morning? I can make you no promises, Xavier. We don't know what this day will bring, but the thought of being apart from you sickens me," I whisper. With all the funeral preparations and spending the day putting up a mental blockade from Shade trying to pry into my thoughts, I tried not to think about my time being up. The days have flown by, and I feel as if I haven't made the most of my time with my family or Xavier.

"It will be fine, Neveah. I won't let anything happen to you. He can't take you from me." Oh, how I wanted to believe him. But like I just said, I couldn't make that promise and neither could he. All I could hope for was that no one else got caught up in this mess and came to harm. I would walk away willingly if it came to protecting my family, I knew that now more than ever. Where could we run where Shade couldn't find us? We couldn't hide out in heaven, and it wasn't the archangel's duty to surround me like bodyguards for the rest of my life. This task was left to me, and I would find a way to lock him in hell so that he can never walk the earth again. But I internalized all those thoughts, and the only thing I could say to Xavier in that moment is that I loved him, and I knew he would do everything in his power to keep me safe.

Even though I knew he couldn't.

There was so much to do this morning and so little time to do it in. I kissed my fiancé and after showering and getting dressed in a lovely long white maxi dress I borrowed from one of my aunts; I went in search of Tia. She was healed on the outside thanks to Xavier and his amazing healing powers, but her spirit animal would take a little longer to heal completely. Unfortunately, there would be no shifting for her for a while. She was so upset last night with almost losing Kes and then waking up to find out we lost Tamara instead. She blamed herself. I blamed myself. There was nothing we could have done, and that is why I was so determined to keep everyone else safe. As I crossed over to her family's wing of the manor, I doubled over in pain from the intense mental bombardment I just received. I was not letting him in, and I have been fighting for days now. I was exhausted and losing the battle.

"Neveah." His voiced rang out loud and clear in my head. *"You will come to me. You are mine now."*

"NO, asshole," I yelled back and closed my eyes, mentally putting my walls back in place.

"Neveah are you alright?" How was I on the floor? I had no idea, I don't remember falling but when I opened my eyes, I saw Tia standing over me. Ugh, and now I was left with a nasty headache.

Tia helped me to stand, and I stumble from the toll that it had just taken on me. My body is spent and with everything that has happened to me this past week, I am in desperate need of a break. Ha, like that would happen. *You're in the thick of it now,* I thought to myself.

"I'm ok, but I need a coffee as big as my face and painkillers are calling my name," I say to her.

She smiles. There's the Tia I need today. "I can definitely help you with all of that. But first, I need to tell you about my weird ass encounter with Eddy earlier."

She fills me in whilst I savor every sip of my coffee and pick at a donut put in front of me by my father. "Eat something," he said in passing and left the room, leaving us to our conversation. I hadn't had an opportunity to find my mother with everything going on yesterday, but I figure with her being in deep discussions with my aunts about the events that have taken place, I am probably the last person she wants to see.

"She is acting very strange, I mean I would be beside myself if anything happened to you, so I almost let it go."

"Let what go?" I said to her, shaking myself from my own thoughts and focusing on what she was saying.

"She was talking about 'she had to do what she promised'. As if she promised something to someone. But then she shifted gears, reminding me of our promise to protect the family. That is not what she was talking about, Neveah, I can feel it."

"Who was she talking about?" I asked, almost whispering it

back to keep our conversation as private as possible in a room full of our family members.

"I don't know. But she ended it with saying she had no choice." She shrugged.

"We will just have to find her after the funeral and have a long talk to her. Maybe it's like you said, and she is just grief stricken and sad. We need to keep her close to us today, she will need us to be strong for her like she has always been for everyone else," I say to her. I feel for Eddy, and I know it is driving her mad with sadness for the loss of Tamara. I would be speaking in riddles too if I was in her shoes.

"I will keep Kes and Siobhan in the loop and we can all be there for her. But Neveah, you don't leave my sight today. You didn't really say what happened to you back there in the hallway, but I am going to take a guess and assume you are being mentally harassed by that dick of a devil." She smiled slightly at her little jab at the end, but it was quickly replaced with her serious face.

"I can't shift, and I need to have my eyes on you at all times. So, I know I am going to possibly fight Xavier for it, but can you at least walk near me in the procession today? It will ease my mind, and my spirit animal is very antsy. I have a feeling—"

I cut her off and grab my cousin's hand. "I will stay close. But I will make no promises and I said the same thing to Xavier this morning, let's just get through this day," I say to her, and she shakes her head at all the things unsaid. I cut her off because I didn't want to admit that I had that same feeling.

25

XAVIER

"So, it appears someone used a charmed artifact to open the barrier the other day. Raphael and I spoke with Willa, and she and the other elders did a quick inventory and found that nothing had been removed from the study. I believe that whoever used this artifact somehow managed to put it back, using the commotion in the manor as a distraction. But that is just my theory. Of course, all the elders swore that no one from the family would dare tamper with the wards and barriers," Michael says to me as I join them at the back of the manor. They had checked every inch of the barrier for discrepancies and found none, which leads them back to someone physically letting the hellhounds through. If Michael's theory is correct, Neveah is not safe, and I need to know what they have planned.

"So, what about Neveah? How do we keep her safe? If someone, and that's a big *if,* was working for Shade, then what's the plan. He told her she only had a week and today is the day that she will have to go with him," I say to him and my father.

"As long as she is within the bounds of the manor, she will be safe," my father pats my shoulder. I know he knows what I am feeling. I need to know she will be ok. Can I protect her from what's to come? I don't know if I am capable, but I will try.

"The chosen can protect herself. She will have to make up her own mind. It is her destiny," Michael says, matter of fact.

"So, you expect her to go with him?" I say to them both. But they don't reply, and that's all the answer I need.

"Why?" I yell. "I was told to protect her; you gave her to me." I make a point to stamp out every word. Why do I feel like I have been set up? I feel like a fool. It's all very clear.

"We didn't expect you to go and fall in love with her, Xavier," Michael spits back. "We gave her to you to protect, yes, but not to marry. So, we allowed you to be engaged and we would have let you get married even, but we knew she wouldn't be able to stay with you. She is God's justice; she is not yours to have."

"Son, it is her destiny. He will find a way to get to her no matter what we do. We must let this play out. We can no longer interfere. It is up to Neveah now," my father says sadly.

"But she is not ready. This is all happening so fast. None of this makes sense. What do you mean we can no longer interfere? You are supposed to help her?" I don't get angry very often, it's just not in my nature, but this all too much to bear.

"We have run out of time, son. Now it is time for you to believe in her. Look at what she did the other day. Trust in her ability to adapt. She is learning as she goes." He reaches in his robes and pulls out a delicate gold chain with a bright blue sapphire pendant attached. "I will leave you with this." He hands it over to me and clasps my hand in his. "Give this to Neveah and tell her to never take it off. It will be your way of finding her no matter where she is." He smiles at me softly. "I will be watching son, we all will." He gives me one last look, expands his wings and takes off into the sky along with the other angels, who were still assisting with fixing the grounds.

"Fear not Xavier, for you still have much to do. She will need you before this is all over and it will be only you who can save her from herself," Michael says, and he takes off to follow the others.

I just stand there for a moment and think about what he just said and how cryptic it was. All I know is that Neveah will not have the help of the angels tonight and we are on our own.

She was never mine to have is all I could think about as I headed back to the manor to find her and get ready for the funeral.

But it wouldn't stop me from loving her.

26

NEV

So, the angels have left. I am on my own. A part of me, on some level, knew that they couldn't protect me from Shade. Something deep inside my soul knew that this was my fight and my fight alone. Alone. But damn, did it suck. I was already searching for Xavier when he found me and told me all that had happened before Michael and Raphael left with the other angels in tow. I tried and failed to put on a brave face, but he could see straight through it.

"Talk to me, Neveah."

"I have been trying to accept all of this for days. I have tried to tell myself that this is what I must do. I have taken all these changes, and I have tried to keep my head held high. But I am terrified, Xavier," I say with trembling hands as he reaches out and grabs them, pulling me into his arms. "I say this to only you because I know you will understand, but if I could run far away from this responsibility, I would do it. But I am here, ready to walk through hell to save anyone else from this fate." There, I have said it. No more. For the first time in my life, I must walk alone without my parents, Tia and Xavier. I take this moment to be sad about everything that I am leaving behind because I know that my life will never be the same from this day forward.

I look at Xavier, and I know there are a million things he wants to say, but instead, he reaches into his pocket and pulls out a beautiful necklace. "A parting gift from my father, he says to never take it off and that wherever you go, I will always find you." He takes the necklace and clasps it around my neck. I gently touch the blue sapphire and am surprised that I can feel it pulsating.

"Like a beacon," I say to him.

"No matter what happens, you will never be lost to me." He takes my hand in his, and he leads me to join the procession outside.

THANK GOODNESS FOR WHITE BECAUSE EVEN WITH THE SUN going down, this Texas heat was not letting up. The entire procession is making its way to our family crypt beyond the back gardens and through the forest. It stands in the middle of a clearing, not too close to the manor and far enough from the barriers so that if something happened, everyone could get back safely. Everyone walked in silence, each with a candle in our hands, and I look ahead to where my uncles and father are carrying Tamara's body; it is like she is floating on the flames. It is crucial that she is surrounded by all the things she loved the most, so Tamara can have them when she passes beyond the veil to heaven—because that's where I know she is going. I smile, remembering Tempest saying that she will undoubtedly want her tablet and cell phone to be up there with her, and my Aunt Penny laughed for the first time in twenty-four hours. Now I see her just up ahead, crying silently in my uncle's arms, and my heart breaks for her. Tamara was her only child. The elders all walk behind them, followed by Eddy and Siobhan, with Tempest walking alone in front of Xavier and me. I glance back, giving Tia and Kes a small smile, with the rest of the family and guests following behind. It's so beautiful seeing all the white and floating candles gracing the sunset sky. It will be dark by the time we get there, and it will indeed be a celebration of light in honor of the precious light we have lost.

∽

My spirit is free, I am everywhere.
In the air that you breathe, in the sounds that you hear,
Please don't cry for me now, my spirit is near.
I'll watch you from the other side,
I'll be the one running, new friends by my side.
Smile at my memory, remember in your heart,
this isn't the end, it's a brand-new start.

TEMPEST WAS THE LAST ONE TO READ HER POEM THAT SHE HAD written in honor of Tamara. The entire service was filled with singing and chanting, all of it to aid in her passing peacefully into the veil of heaven. The angels would be waiting to guide my cousin into her next life beyond her earthly body. That's what my family always believed and taught us when it came to the death of a loved one. I can feel the weight of everyone's emotions all around me, and the air is thick with grief. Looking over at Eddy, I can see that she is barely able to stand anymore. Tia and Siobhan are both holding her up, consoling her, and it broke me to see her so broken. My mother replaced Tempest at the podium to do one more spell, and then the service would be complete. She raises her hands high, and we extend our candles as she begins to speak. "Conservationem corporis, exaltatio spiritus, tutela animam," we repeat the chant and blow out our candles. Tamara's body will be preserved without decay for ten days to allow her parents to visit and mourn. She will then be removed from the funeral platform and placed in her final resting place in our family crypt. It was all so final, and I felt that finality in more ways than one. I can feel the constant telepathic poking that Shade was doing, and it is beginning to wear me down. It takes everything in me to hold him at bay, and the last thing I want to do is worry Xavier or anyone else, considering the circumstance. As our family and friends mingle and speak words of encouragement and condolences to one another, I can see that there have been torches lit to guide everyone safely back to the manor. I take stock of everyone around me as we begin our walk back. Quickly glancing over my shoulder toward the funeral platform, I see my Aunt Penny hugging Eddy and walking away, leaving her alone to be with Tamara.

"Hey, guys, I am going to sit with Eddy for a minute, and I will walk back with her to the manor."

"Do you want us to stay with you?" Tia said to me as I turn to walk away from them. I know that the last thing she wants to do is leave my side, and by the look on Xavier's face, he didn't either. But there is no reason for me to be concerned; all the wards and barriers have been double-checked by the angels before they left. I am keeping Shade at bay telepathically, and I have hope that he will be a problem for another day.

"I will be fine. I don't want her to be alone, and I am safe with Eddy by my side," I say to them as I walk away.

I walk over to Eddy and sit next to her, and we just sit in silence for a while. I can still hear the faint chatter from all of our family and friends in the distance when she finally decides to speak.

"I'm not ok if that's what you're going to ask me. Tamara was my responsibility, and I ultimately failed her."

"How were you to know Eddy? We were all fighting out there, and with all the chaos, none of us saw her," I said to her gently. I didn't want to upset her further, and I didn't want to make this about me. I felt the same guilt.

I sit closer to Eddy and pull her into a hug as she breaks down again on my shoulder. This is going to eat at her for a very long time. I don't think the elders will assign anyone new to her, and maybe that is a good thing. She will need a lot of time to heal and stop blaming herself for what happened to her sister witch.

"I never meant for this to happen. But I had no choice. I had to protect—Shade gave me no choice." I can barely understand what she is saying; she was crying so hard. I wonder if this is what she was trying to tell Tia this morning.

"Who, Eddy?" I ask her, but she just kept sobbing into my shoulder and babbling.

"He promised that if I did what he asked, he would leave us alone." I heard that last bit loud and clear.

"Eddy, who is he?" I say slowly. I instantly go on alert and notice that it is completely silent all around us.

"Don't you see that I have to deliver you to him," she says as she lifts her head off my shoulder and wipes her tears. I have never seen her look so lost.

"He will take the baby away from me, and that can't happen, Neveah. He is the future." Eddy stands and takes one last look at Tamara, and then she turns to face me.

"Wait, what?" I am confused. Is she saying what I think she is saying? Then it hits me, and it all becomes clear. Shade has been using her to get to me, and he has threatened her unborn child to do it. Eddy is as much a part of this prophecy as I am. She would never betray our family or me, but she has no choice at the risk of losing the first male child born into our family.

"Eddy, you're pregnant," I say to her with a bit of excitement in my voice. I don't want her to know that I am worried or that I am trying to keep her talking to figure out a way to get away from her.

"I found out a few weeks ago," she says absently. "I was further along than they thought, and that's when they told me it is a boy."

"Eddy, why didn't you just tell elder? You'll be more protected than me. He is the future." I need to change tactics. "No more sacrifices; you've done enough for our family. You can raise your son in peace. Hell, my mother would move you to the manor permanently. For him, let me make the sacrifice. I will go willingly. I will cross the barrier and go to Shade. Let me just go and say goodbye first," I plead.

"See, you get it now. You are the chosen, and you are the sacrifice." She shakes her head at me, eyes wild and desperate. I feel for her.

"I do," I say to her, but just as I am about to launch myself in the air, I'm struck with another severe telepathic attack that brings me to my knee. This one catches me off guard; I was so focused on Eddy I must have let down my walls. The pain is so bad, but still, I try to scramble to my feet. The last thing I want to do is pass out. I can't allow myself to be that vulnerable.

"I don't think saying goodbye would be wise. We both know Tia would not allow you to give yourself up, and neither would Xavier. Make this easy on them, Neveah." She walks over to where I am trying to stand, but I can't seem to get my feet under me.

"Eddy, please," I implore her. I just want to do this on my own terms. I just want to see Xavier and tell Tia it will all be ok. I try to get up once more, but I feel a pinch on the side of my neck. Did she just stick me with something? I can feel my walls come crashing down around me.

"It's just a sedative; you will be fine, I promise." I hear Eddy say, but she sounds so far away.

The last thing I hear before I pass out is Eddy crying again.

EPILOGUE

EDDY

I watched as Shade took Neveah and vanished. Our deal is done. My son would be saved. My life as I knew it was over; I betrayed my family and gave my own over to the devil himself. If the circumstances had been any different, I would have died to protect Neveah, and I would have never given her over to him. My very principles had been snatched away from me the moment he appeared out of thin air and threatened the life of my unborn son. I didn't even get a chance to tell the elders, let alone formulate a plan that involved not betraying my cousin. Tia will never forgive me; none of the shifters will. It is our duty to protect our sisters, and yet I failed… twice. The last moment with Tamara as she lay dead on that platform will hunt me for the rest of my life, and so would my betrayal of Neveah. So, I have to put as much distance between me and the manor as possible. It wouldn't take long for them to realize that I was the one who used the stone used to disrupt the barrier. I was the one that gave Neveah over. I was the traitor, and they would come to find me. If you had told me months ago that a one-night stand would lead me to this exact moment, I would have laughed and maybe even let my spirit animal maul the person for being crazy. But this is my reality, and I will run until I can't run anymore.

TO BE CONTINUED....

Join me for the continuation of the story in
Temptation
(Owensen Witches series Book 2)
PREORDER NOW

THANK YOU!!

To all the readers who stumbled upon this book and decided to give it a go...whether you loved it or not, I thank you.

To my brainstorming muse of a sister Fawn, you keep my wheels turning. I would be a mess of ideas without you.

To my husband and son Bryce for just being patient.... you're my heroes. I love you both.

Big thanks to Jade Mills of Between the Emerald Page for your super-duper editing. You are amazing.

To the Owens/Lewis family for inspiring me to tell this tale.

ABOUT THE AUTHOR

I am Undreia Capewell (pen name Dreia Wells) and I was born and raised in Houston, Texas but live with my husband and son in England. I love books and I always dreamed of writing my own one day. I love a good story and I hope (crossing my fingers) that you will enjoy my first book of my first ever series. I write mostly Fantasy/Paranormal Romance but who knows where it all may lead. Check me out on Social media...go ahead Stalk away.

Stay in touch

Join her reader group Dreia Wells and all her crazy!!

Sign up to my Newsletter:

https://www.subscribepage.com/w5y8y0

instagram.com/dreia_wells_author

ALSO BY DREIA WELLS

OWENSEN WITCHES SERIES

CHOSEN

TEMPTATION

Printed in Great Britain
by Amazon

68035545R00073